Cashmere Mafia

By: Keisha R. Ervin

Table of Content

Everybody in this club got a smile up on they face and I'm hatin' on the low.

-Chris, "Twerkin' In My Heels"

Chapter 1

If I have to spend one more New Year's Eve in the club wit' a bunch of drunk and in-love muthafucka's I'ma kill myself! Every year it's the same ole tired scene; me standing in the center of the club at the stroke of midnight nursing a half empty glass of champagne while the couples surrounding me tongue each other down like it's their last day on earth. I swear to god I am over it! I mean, when is it going to be my turn to be so in-love that the people around me get jealous?

I wanna walk down the aisle and say "I Do" to my prince charming but no, here I am thirty, wit' no kids, a great job and a fat ass wit' no man. I've done everything I can think of to find my one and only. I've gone to church, the club, Home Depot, Foot Locker, sports games, prayed to Jesus, Allah, Oprah and Gayle and still I'm single. I swear I don't know how much more I can take.

I come from a famous bloodline, I'm rich, successful and if I must say drop dead gorgeous but none of that matters when I slip underneath the covers and go to bed alone at night. Oh, and who am I? Forgive me for being rude. I'm Sunday Rose Vasi. Most people know me because I'm a highly successful matchmaker. Others know me because of my famous grandmother the jazz great Dahl Monroe or my ubber stylish and equally famous cousin Dylan Dahl Monroe Carter.

Sure, on the outside looking in I have it all but hell I'm like my girl Jill Scott. I can buy my own house, car and kill a spider above my bed but I still need a man. And yeah, I can buy 50 million mechanical devices to rock my pussy to sleep but ain't nothin' and I mean nothin' like having a big, strong, fine ass man in-between my legs. Unlike Chilli from the group TLC I don't have a checklist. At this point, I'll take anything wit' a pulse and paycheck. I'm not too hard to please.

All I want is to be loved unconditionally, get married and start a family. Is that asking for too much? I personally don't think so. What I do know is that this will be the last New Years Eve I spend alone. It is officially

January 1, 2014 and I am making a solemn vow that by December 31st I will have a man. The question is how do I find him? Because sitting around and waiting on him to find me is not and option anymore. Thirty years of waiting has been long enough. It's time to get this show on the road but before operation find me a man begins, I'ma head home, take off these tight ass Spanx, eat me a bowl of cereal and take my ass to bed.

After ten years of living in L.A. I'm moving back home to St. Louis to start the second branch of my matchmaking company *Two Hearts*. After years of unsuccessful dating, I decided that I'd pretty much ran the gamut on dating and that I would be an expert on setting other love sick souls like myself up on dates. Well, my theory proved to be right because I have a 90% success rate with my clients, a weekly column in Cosmopolitan magazine and an offer on the table for my very own reality show.

Like most women after being so focused on my career, one day I woke up and realized that I was thirty with a non existent personal life and that I hadn't had sex in over a year! I know pitiful, right but that's what happens when you're trying to be superwoman. It doesn't help much either that most men find me to be brash and tightly wound but after you've been through the hell I've been through with family and dating you'd be that way too.

It's my first week back in St. Louis and my mother Lane is throwing me a welcome home dinner. I honestly don't know why I'm even gonna put myself through the torture of going. Nothing ever changes. As soon as I walk into my mother's home she's gonna make a comment about my weight, ask if I'm still single and compare me to my twin brother the rest of the day. If it wasn't for my brother formerly known as Seth and my cousin Dylan, I swear Sunday dinner would not be a priority on my list. Before I go into this house let me tell you a little bit about my family. If you look up the definition of modern family you will see a big picture of us.

My mother although born and raised in St. Louis talks and acts like she's a character from Gone With The Wind. It's so annoying and I would never admit it to her face but my mother's fake southern charm is what gives her character. My twin brother Seth aka Teyana aka Tee-Tee aka Easy-Breezy-Beautiful-Bad-Bitch is flamboyantly gay and on top of that married wit' a baby! Yes, even my brother has a man and I don't.

Although my brother gets on my last nerve sometimes I totally adore him, his husband Bernard and their baby girl Princess Gaga. Uh huh, you read it right. My nieces name is absolutely ridiculous but let's move on. Tee-Tee is my absolute best friend. I love him dearly. When he was mocked for being gay and wearing women's clothing I was his shoulder to cry on. We've been through the storm together and I would give my life for him.

I'm totally J as in jealous of my brother and his cute little family but if my plan goes as I pray it will, I'll have a ring on my left hand too. Now that I've brought you up to speed on everything let me take my ass into this house. It's cold as hell outside. As I walk into my moms sprawling estate located in the Forest Park section of St. Louis, I take a deep breath and prepare myself for war.

"Hi yu doing, Sunday?" Our family's maid Rosa says as she greets me at the door.

"Fine, Rosa and you?" I respond as she takes my coat.

"Oh, I'm doing fine. Jur mother drive me crazy as always but I'm okay," Rosa smiles.

"Where is everybody?" I ask, looking around.

"They're in the dining room."

"Thanks Rosa."

As my six inch heels click against the marble floor a sense of dread rushes over me. My mother is going to lose her shit once she hears my news. I can't even front though apart of me can't wait to see the look of shock on her face when I tell her what my plans are.

"Hey everybody!" I say as I enter the dining area.

Everybody's there Tee-Tee, Bernard, Princess Gaga, Dylan, Angel and Mason. My aunt Candy, who is Dylan's mother, has never been to Sunday dinner due to the fact that she and my mother don't get along but I'll tell you more about that later.

"Welcome home!" Everyone jumps up to greet me.

"Now you know you wrong for that?" My mother tunes up her face and looks at me.

"Don't start wit' me mama." I give her the evil eye as I air-kiss my cousin Dylan on the cheek.

"I'm just saying spandex ain't meant for everybody." She bucks her eyes and takes a sip of wine.

I so wanna tell my mother that the skin underneath her eyes is starting to look like Hugh Hefner's ball sack but that would be inappropriate so instead I say, "And you're the best looking gay guy here mother."

"Bloop!" Tee-Tee points his finger at her. "She told you. Don't mind her Sunday you look cute as always." Tee-Tee assures me.

"I know I do," I scoff.

Shit, I don't know what my mama trippin' off of. I look good. Scratch that I look better than good. I look better than Beyoncé wit' a sickening sew-in and a dope ass pair of Louboutin heels. I am slayin' the scene in a black motorcycle leather jacket, white deep v-neck tee shirt, red patent leather not spandex Dolce & Gabbana skinny pants and black pointed toe Givenchy pumps. Yes, I am a size 13 but I am fierce honey wit' a capital F. All of my curves are in the right place.

Look, let me break down my physique for you real quick so we can continue. I'm 5'5 with butter colored skin. I have shoulder length curly honey blonde hair, almond shaped, crystal clear blue eyes, cheekbones like Naomi Campbell and Playboy bunny full pink lips. My tits are a 37DD, my stomach is flat and I have hips and ass for days and whoever has a problem wit' me dressing like the diva I am and not like a basic bitch can eat a dick wit' duck sauce. Now let's continue.

"Have a seat dear." My mother nods her head towards a seat next her. "Dinner is about to start."

Even though my mother sometimes acts like a descendant of the devil I must admit that she's beyond beautiful. Her skin is the color of the sun while her tranquilizing, cat-shaped blue eyes capture your soul every time you look at her. To be 50 years old my mother has it going on. Her waist is still a slim size 6 and she normally rocked her long brown and golden blonde hair in a chic layered do. But today she had on a wig that was black and styled in a chic bob with bangs.

Even though she and I don't share the same taste in home décor my mother keeps her house immaculate. Her entire home was featured in Elle Décor magazine. Her house has a very traditional feel to it but there are some modern touches. For instance the dining room ceiling is painted white but then the walls are a striking pear green shade. A floor to ceiling window with black and white paisley drapes overlooking the Olympic size pool in the backyard sits in front of the dining room table. The twelve seat wooden dining table is my mothers pride and joy. It was passed down to her from my grandmother Dahl. The rest of the room consists of a Swarovski crystal chandelier and original paintings by her favorite artist.

"How about today you start off with a nice sensible salad dear?" My mother starts in.

"No, thank you." I sat down and placed my napkin over my lap.

"But honey you need to. I know you don't wanna end up looking like Precious," she giggled.

"If I wanted a salad I would have Chef make me a salad," I stress becoming annoyed.

"*Okay* a second on the lips last forever on the hips." She mumbles loud enough for me to hear.

For once I'm not gonna even respond. I'ma just pretend that I was raised by a normal mother and not one who was raised by wolves.

"Leave her alone Lane." My father Eric said as he entered the room.

Oh, did I forget to mention that my parents are divorced. After twenty years of marriage, my father grew tired of living the façade that he and my mother were happily married and filed for divorce. A year late, he started to date a girl name ZaShontay who is five years younger than me might I add. Despite my father's lapse in judgment I love him dearly and we are extremely close. No matter what, I can always expect to have my fathers support.

"Now on to pressing matters." My mother situated herself in her seat as Rosa brought out our first course. "The Pink Hats our having our annual auction next week and I need to know what you all will be auctioning off."

"I got a Keri Hilson tee-shirt I can donate," Tee-Tee jokingly replied.

"Oh no you won't," Bernard snapped. "That's my damn shirt."

"No need to bicker. That won't be necessary Tee-Tee." My mother kindly patted him on the back of his hand.

"I was just playin' boo." Tee-Tee rubbed Bernard back. "Calm down. No seriously, I'll think of something mama." He promised.

"I'll donate some of my cookbooks and a chance to win a guest spot on my cooking show," Dylan offered.

"Oh that's a great idea Dylan. The ladies will love that." My mother clapped, excitedly.

"And I can sign a pair of my boxing gloves and trunks," Angel added.

"Wonderful and what about you, dear?" My mother said, referring to me.

"How about I donate these Dolce & Gabbana pants I have on?" I quipped, trying to piss her off.

"Sweetie nobody not even a hooker wants those pants." My mother laughed taking another sip of her drink.

"I mean no wonder you're still single. Who wants to marry a woman walking around wearing spandex pants?"

"Their patent leather," I yell. "Patent leather, patent leather, patent leather!"

"Don't get mad at me 'cause you can't keep a man."

"If you would've stayed with Damon like I told you to you would be married with kids by now," Tee-Tee added salt to my game.

"Oooooooooh, no she didn't." Dylan fanned herself with her napkin.

Okay, see my brother has gone cray-cray. Damon was my ex-boyfriend. He and I were together all through high school and our first two years of college. When we were twenty I found out that not only was he cheating on me but that he'd gotten another chick pregnant. To say that I was devastated is an understatement. I was emotionally demolished. I thought I was going to marry this man. I tried so hard to forgive him and move on as if nothing had happened but there was no way on gods green earth that I could look at him and his betrayal in the face on a daily basis and keep my sanity.

My brother said I was a fool for leaving him because according to him all men cheat. I however did not intend on spending the rest of my life living a lie just for appearances sake. No, I would be happy or die trying.

"Tee-Tee, I've told you this before if you love Damon so much why don't you marry him?" I rolled my neck.

"Baby Damon can't handle all of this." He rolled his torso like a snake.

Oh my god I'ma throw up.

"On that note I have a request of all of you, except for mama and Tee-Tee." I hold up my hand to block her face.

"Anything for you boo boo." Dylan winked her eye.

"Okay check it. Ya'll know I ain't got no man and ain't seen no part of one since Tiger Woods got caught cheating."

"You ain't never lied about that!" My mother laughed into her glass.

"Anyway!" I rolled my eyes so hard at her I thought they were going to fall out. "Well, I have a plan. Since ya'll know me so well I figured I'd ask each of you to set me up on a date. I mean out of the four of you I should be able to meet Mr. Right. It's a new year and a new day and I have vowed to meet my boo by the end of the year but if I don't, I've decided." I paused for dramatic effect.

"If by chance, I don't find the love my life, I have frozen my eggs and this time next year I will be starting IVF treatments in order to have a baby." I looked directly at my mother with glee.

"Well hit me over the head wit' a shovel." She sat up straight. "Girl, have you lost your damn mind?"

"No mama, have you?" I cocked my head to the side.

"I swear your life's mission is to send me to an early grave." She took a huge gulp of wine.

"You're right mama. Everyday I dream of your demise." I shot her devilish grin.

"Why can't you wait until you meet the right person?'

ears old, mother. I'm not

she waved me off. "30 ain't shit. I'm
. summoned Rosa for another drink.

don't understand where I went wrong with
ou trying to make me the laughing stock of St.
L.   Why can't you be more like your brother?" My
mother declared as Rosa refilled her wine glass.

"'Cause I'm me mother and the faster you accept
that the better off we'll be."

"I think it's a fantastic idea." Tee-Tee chimed in. "I
already know the perfect guy."

"Me too," Dylan beamed. "As a matter of fact, I
know I have the perfect guy for you, right baby?" She
nudged Angel with her elbow.

"Oh yeah, ole boy would be perfect," he agreed.

"You can meet him this Friday," Dylan continued.

"Sounds like a plan to me." I scrunched up my nose
at my mother and took a huge bite of steak.

19

Boy you talk a lot of shit.

-Chris, "Concrete"

Chapter 2

So, I thought after asking my lovely family to hook me up with my husband-to-be that I'd never have to step foot in the club again. Yet, I find myself walking into The City night club at eleven o'clock on a Saturday night with Tee-Tee and Dylan.

"Dylan, explain to me why I'm meeting this guy at the club and why are you and Tee-Tee chaperoning? What happened to dinner and a movie?"

"Well..." she replied, with a look of dread on her face.

"What Dylan? You're scaring me. Who is this guy and why won't you tell me anything about him?" I crossed my arms across my chest.

"You'll find out soon enough. Come on." She took me by the hand led me inside the club.

As soon as I step foot inside The City, I felt as if I've been transported into a galaxy filled with neon strobe lights and bass filled, booty-bouncin' music. The club might not be the best place to find a man but it sure is the place to release your inhibitions and let go. But tonight I can't seem to let loose. The thought of meeting my first blind date is wreaking havoc on my nerves so I decide to head to over to the private bar for the V.I.P. guests. With a glass of champagne in my system I begin to relax. I just hope whoever this mystery man is, that I'll like him so this journey can be over quickly. It's gonna take at least a year to plan our wedding.

"Where is this guy at? We've been waiting for over an hour?" I asked, glancing at my Cartier watch.

"Does it matter?" Tee-Tee replied. "We snatchin' wigs tonight, girl! Can't none of these hoes in here fuck wit' us. You better stand up and let'em know!" He waved his hand in the air while popping his butt to the beat.

"Stop you gon' make me choke on my drink." I laughed as a crowd of women ran over to the V.I.P section, where we were sitting. "What is going on?"

"Your blind date is here," Dylan said into my ear.

22

"Ladies and gentleman ya' boy Blue is in the building!" The DJ announced to the crowd. "It's time to turn up!"

Before I could even blink, Blue and an entourage of about fifteen niggas walked into the club. Although I don't date industry dudes I can't even deny that Blue's swagger is off the charts. He's a Grammy award winning rapper and songwriter whose sold over twenty million records worldwide and been featured in Forbes, XXL, GQ and Vogue magazine.

The blogs and tabloids pegged him to be the George Clooney of hip hop. He never stuck to one woman for too long. He's been linked to Khloe Kardashian, Sanaa Lathan and Rihanna. Blue has also had multiple run-ins with the law. His quick temper and I don't give a fuck attitude has gotten him in a lot of trouble. But to see him up close I start to understand why he can't be tamed. Fine isn't the word to describe him. He's dangerously sexy. He's about six feet four in height, two and forty hundred pounds in weight and had skin the shade of honey. The man's body was rock solid. He rocked a low cut with spinning waves, had thick eyebrows, smoldering hazel eyes, a thick luscious beard and kissable full lips.

An uncountable amount of tattoos filled his neck, chest and arms. He even had the letters STL tatted on his left cheek. The black snapback with the word Nice written across it, black Ray-Ban shades, black sweatshirt, tan cargo pants and Air Jordan 3's enhanced his muscular frame. I don't know how Blue did it but upon sight, I melted and had an orgasm, at the same damn time.

Homeboy was sexy as hell. He was tall and cocky just how I liked'em. Blue had that bad boy swagger that I secretly lusted after but was too emotional scared to date. See me and industry cats don't mix. Industry dudes are full of shit and too full of themselves. All they do is fuck chick after chick. I don't have time for that. Besides that, my mama and my daddy would kill me if I bought a dude like Blue home. Well hell, maybe that isn't such a bad idea. I would love to be the one to give my mother the long-awaited heart attack she'd been begging for.

However, there was no need getting my panties moist over Blue. He was way too flashy and I was so unbothered by the glitz and glamour of being in the lime light. I tried my hardest to stay under the radar which never seemed to work. I hated to be the center of attention. With a look of horror on my face I watched as Blue made his way through the club. I was completely outdone at the females in the club.

They were losing their mind over him. Chicks were straight screaming, jumping up and down, waving their hands, blowing kisses, bending over and twerkin' their ass just to get his attention. I mean he was fine and all but goddamn. I would never sweat any dude that hard. Blue seemed completely unfazed by it all. He had a stone expression on his face as he and his crew took over the V.I.P area. Spotting Dylan, he quickly came over to show her love.

"What up Dylan?" Blue hugged her tight.

"Hey baby." She hugged him back.

"Thanks for coming out. Where my man Angel at?" Blue looked around for him.

"He's at home with our son. He told me to tell you what's up," Dylan replied. "But let me introduce you to my cousin that I was telling you about. Blue, this is Sunday

Rose. Sunday, this is Blue," Dylan smiled, pleased with herself.

Blue and I locked eyes with one another and I could tell by the smirk on his face that he liked what he saw. I was killin'em in a black fitted crop top, red midi skirt, black socks pushed down and Jeffrey Campbell's remixed version of the Timberland boot. I was serving tits and ass for days. I kept it cool though and kept a straight face. He might've liked what he saw but I wasn't thirsty for any attention from him.

"How you doing, miss lady?" Blue extended his hand for a shake.

"Hello," I replied, placing my stiletto nailed hand inside his.

"So you're the infamous Sunday Rose, I've been hearing so much about." Blue admired my curvaceous frame. "I see you."

"I know you do," I countered.

"Blue," Tee-Tee chimed in standing up.

The freak'um dress he was wearing was so tight it barely covered his ass.

"I'm Tee-Tee," he continued. "Aka Bang Me All Night Long." Tee-Tee ran his tongue across his upper lip, flirtatiously.

"Yo' who the fuck is this? Yo' homeboy need to chill." Blue eyed Dylan quizzically.

"I'm sorry," she apologized. "If you don't quit!" Dylan insisted, stomping her foot.

"Huuuuh, it's always my fault.com," Tee-Tee groaned, plopping back down.

"Ya'll drinking?" Blue shouted over the loud music.

"Hell yeah," Dylan exclaimed. "I'm off mommy duty tonight. I'm trying to kick it."

"Sunday you want another drink?" Blue asked as several waitresses bought over ice filled buckets of Ciroc, Ace of Spades, Patron and Grand Marnier.

"No, I'm good." I held up my glass of champagne.

"I should've known. Stick wit' that pretty girl drink. You ain't bout that life," Blue laughed with his homeboys.

Did this nigga just try me? 'Cause I really think he just came for my throat. See this dude got me fucked up. I might be a little prissy and well put together but I was the kind of girl that never backed down from a challenge.

"What's that supposed to mean?" I asked, cocking my head to the side.

"It means you look like one of them bougie boards that don't drink hard liquor. I bet all you drink is champagne and wine spritzer." Blue shot back.

"That's the funny thing about looks. Looks can be very deceiving." I rose from my seat and got in his face

Our lips were inches apart.

"I'll take a shot of Patron, please."

"You sure you wanna do that?" Blue looked me square in the eyes.

His menacing gaze was so intense it felt like we were physically touching. Staring into his eyes I felt small, like a little girl. I didn't like it at all. I'm always in control

28

of my feelings so how dare this fine muthafucka me feel otherwise.

"No, the question is do you know who you're fuckin' wit 'cause I'm not the one boo-boo."

"And I ain't no lame ass nigga so since you talkin' all that big girl shit, let's see if you can sit at the grown folks table. Let's see who can out drink who. If I win you give me your number," Blue challenged.

"And if I win... how about I don't give you my number," I opposed.

"Bet. Get ready to lose miss lady. Ay yo let me get two Fireballs." Blue had the bartender pour us both a shot.

"Girl, what the hell are you doing?" Tee-Tee hissed in my ear. "You know yo' ass don't drink like that."

"I got this." I smiled and winked my eye at my brother.

Then the bartender handed Blue and I a small shot glass full of the cinnamon flavored whisky. What surprised me was that the top was set on fire.

"What in the Samuel L. Jackson is this?" I turned and asked Dylan.

"It's a Fireball," she explained.

"I know that but what is it? All I see is fire and I'm not drinking no damn fire," I exclaimed. "I like my insides."

"You backing out already miss lady?" Blue swallowed his shot in one swift drink.

"Never. I ain't no punk." I inhaled deep,

Okay Sunday, you can do this. You are not a lame. You're a fearless woman. Remember what Beyoncé said. You are flawless. As I called on the spirits of Whitney and Biggie, I closed my eyes tight and drank the potent liquor. The smooth sensation of the whiskey burned the fuck outta my throat! The non existent singer career I had was over.

Five Fireball shots later, I was leaning. I was starting to sweat and pretty girls don't sweat, we glisten. It was literally taking the will of Blue Ivy for me not to pass out. I didn't have it in me to take another sip let alone a whole drink.

"Uh oh! You give up?" Blue questioned, grinning.

The smug look on his face burned me up and inside. I couldn't let him win. His fine ass had to be brought down a peg or two.

"Gon' ahead and tape out. I still might take you out for dinner tomor." He said with a laugh.

"You know what? For a minute there I almost forgot how bad your personality was." I replied, sarcastically. "I don't lose boo-boo."

I swallowed the throw up in the back of my throat and gulped down the drink.

"That's my bitch!" Tee-Tee pointed his finger in the air.

For the next hour Blue and I went shot for shot. Everyone surrounded us, dying to see who would be the first to break. His people and my people cheered us on. He didn't back down and neither did I. I was determined not to be the first one to fold.

"You good, homeboy?" I teased, holding up my shot glass.

31

The room was tilted and I felt off kilter but I had a damn point to prove to this arrogant muthafucka. I watched as Blue eyed the next shot with pure contempt.

"Yo', I'm done." He bowed out, waving his hands. "Yo' ass is crazy. Yo Dylan yo' cousin is a live one." Blue held his head.

"I told you I would win!" I pushed Tee-Tee playfully. "Ya'll ready?" I said picking up my Stella McCartney clutch.

"You are freakin' insane." Dylan said, astonished.

"Aye, where you going?" Blue grabbed my hand before I could leave.

"I'm going to the mountain." I tried not to slur my words but failed. "I mean home," I giggled.

"On some real shit. Give me your number." He got up in my personal space.

"No... a bet is a bet." I grinned then breezed out of the club before he could stop me again.

Outside in the cold, brisk, winter air the rapid wind nearly knocked my drunk ass over.

"You betta hope yo' ass don't have alcohol poisoning 'cause I ain't about that waiting room life," Tee-Tee scolded me while helping me into my jacket.

"Blah-blah-blah-blah! I'm drunk as fuuuuuuuuuuuuuck." I leaned forward and ran my index finger down my brothers' lips.

"Does this bitch not realize I will fight her? If you don't get yo' drink ass off of me." He made me stand up straight.

"Can't keep yo' eyes off my fatty daddy!" I sang slapping my own ass.

"She can not drive herself home. We're gonna have to take her home," Dylan added.

"Ya'll some haters! Haters with a capital K! Haaaaaaaa! I messed up!" I stumbled back and forth.

"Uh oh." I stopped mid-stride. "I think I just pee'd a little bit."

"Oh honey… I won't tell anyone," Dylan assured, feeling sorry for me.

33

"He thought he was gon' win but he didn't!" I hiccupped.

"I won! I won! I shot the bee-bee gun! He lost! He lost! He ate tomato sauce! These niggas ain't got shit on me! I'm the muthafuckin' king of the world!" I yelled to the sky, spinning around in a circle.

Then everything went black.

"I don't hate you 'cause you're fat. You're fat 'cause I hate you.

"Mean Girls"

Chapter 3

"Oh my god," I groaned, waking up from a deep sleep.

The nonstop sound of my iPhone ringing was driving me freaking insane. *Who in the hell keeps on calling me?* I swear somebody old better have died or Beyoncé concert tickets have gone on sale. Other than that, whoever keeps blowing up my phone while I'm nursing a hangover is going to get cussed the fuck out. Reeking of liquor, I reached over and picked up my cell phone. It was my brother calling.

"Whaaaaaat?" I held my head as the room spun out of control.

"Where the hell are you at?"

"I'm at home in bed. Where else would I be?" I lay my head back on the pillow and closed my eyes.

Even with my eyes closed the room was still spinning.

"Mama is having a conniption fit, girl. You have already missed the first half of the auction. You betta get here before intermission or I won't be responsible for what mama is going to do to you. You know she's been known to castrate fools." Tee-Tee shrilled into the phone.

"Get yo' drunk ass here now!" He hung up on me.

Rolling my eyes, I threw my phone down. Everything on my face felt crusty. My mouth tasted like I'd had the whole Miami Heats' roaster of dicks in my mouth. Lord knows, I hadn't sucked a dick since Chanté Moore had a hit. There was no way I was going to make it to the auction. I wasn't in the mood to be smiling and faking like I liked those stuffy broads.

But if I didn't go I'd never hear the end of it from mama. She'd hold it over my head for the rest of my life. I didn't need that bitter old woman on my back so I threw the comfy covers off of my body. It took me at least ten minutes to get from my bed to the master bathroom which was only steps away.

When I finally got inside the bathroom and flicked on the light I was scared shitless at my reflection in the mirror. I looked like dog shit. My eyes had dark circles around them and smeared eye liner was all over my dry face. There were gooey eye boogers in the corners of my eyes. My entire body felt like I'd been ran over by a Mack truck.

"Jesus be a fence," I prayed.

I honestly don't know how Anna Nicole did it. Being a sloppy drunk is not my cup of tea. I promise I will never touch another drink in my life. After brushing my teeth and taking a much needed shower, I shuffled slowly over to my walk-in closet and picked out a sliver sequined jacket, white button up shirt, skin tight white cigarette pants, tan single sole Manolo Blahnik heels and a pair of black Balenciaga Aviator shades.

With the way I feel, this will most certainly be a no makeup kind of day. Dressed, I threw my hair back into a messy ponytail, grabbed my clutch purse, car keys and rushed out of the door. But to my chagrin as soon as I got outside of my building, I realized that my Mercedes Benz SLS AMG GT Coupe wasn't there.

"Where the fuck is my car?" I shrieked in a panic. "Lord, Jesus, my car has been stolen!" I took my phone out of my purse to call the police.

Before I could press the number 9 a text message from Tee-Tee came through.

Today 4.05PM

Your car is still at the club. Take a cab here and we'll go pick it up afterwards.

"Why Lord? Why?" I yelled to the heavens.

It took twenty minutes just for a cab to come and when it did the inside smelled like sour booty crack and leftover Chinese takeout. I swear the universe is repaying me for some shit I did in a past life. I'd never been so happy to see the Westborough Country Club. My family had been active members for three generations. Growing up, I always hated going to the country club. Some of my worst childhood memories stemmed from that place. But I frankly don't feel dredging up a bunch of old shit so we'll talk about that later. Inside the country club I was escorted to the banquet hall. Tee-Tee was at the door waiting my arrival.

"You're here just in time. Intermission is almost over." He handed me a program. "But girl. What did you do get dressed in the dark?"

I looked down at my outfit and noticed that my shirt was wrinkled and wasn't buttoned up correctly. I didn't even have on matching shoes.

"Shit!" I began to unbutton my shirt. "Where's mama?" I spoke at once.

"Oh shit. She's coming our way now. Try not to look so hung-over." Tee-Tee helped me fix my disheveled clothes.

My mother made her way through each table with a forced smile on her face. Lane was all about appearances so there was no way that she was going to let the other women know that there was trouble on the horizon.

"Where in hell have you been?" My mother grimaced, pulling me outside the banquet doors.

"I over slept mama," I said, buttoning up my shirt correctly.

"And why do you look like Lindsay Lohan after one of her arrest?" My mother eyed me quizzically.

After a second she stepped back.

"My god you're drunk," she gasped.

"Technically I'm hung-over," I laughed.

"Why is everything a joke with you? All I asked was that you come and support me and this is how you show up." She looked me up and down with disgust. "And you don't even have the color pink on."

Using my index finger, I tilted my shades down and noticed that all of the ladies wore pink outfits with matching pink hats. It was like a bottle of Pepto Bismol had exploded all over the room. There were pink linens on the tables, pink flowers and pink napkins. Seeing so much pink all at once made me want to vomit.

"I don't have time for this. Have a seat with your brother and please stay out of trouble." My mother warned before storming back inside.

41

"Well that went better than I expected," Tee-Tee joked. "C'mon, Dylan is waiting for us at our table. We're sitting with Mrs. Mary Beth and Mrs. Claudette."

"Oh lord," I groaned.

On my way to the table I noticed all of my mothers' friends and some of their daughters, stare, whisper and snicker as I walked by. I couldn't help but be ignorant and stick my tongue out them.

"Sunday Rose is that you?" Mrs. Claudette smiled, brightly.

"Yes ma'am, it's me." I struggled not to throw up the liquor from the night before.

"Chile, I haven't seen you in a month of Sunday's. Let me take a look at you." She gave me a once over glance. "I see you got that weight up off you, good girl. You look a lot better now."

"Thank you," I replied, trying my damnest to keep my composure.

I absolutely hate when old people give backhanded compliments. Mrs. Claudette did not know me. I will check an old bitch. Her old ass could get it just like everybody else.

"Mrs. Mary Beth, how are you?" I spoke taking off my shades.

"Living," she responded curtly, fanning herself with a program.

I was never going to win with these old Betty's so I sat my ass down and made a vow to ignore them for the rest of the afternoon.

"Girl, you look like shit." Dylan said, as I sat beside her.

"Why are you talkin' so loud?" I covered my ears. "Use your inside voice please."

"I am el'drunko."

"Whatever," I sighed, signaling for a waitress.

I know I said I was never drinking again but I needed all of the liquid courage in the world to get through this fiasco.

"Yes." The young girl responded.

"Can I have a Bloody Mary, please?"

"Mama is gon' kill you," Tee-Tee chuckled.

"What's new," I replied, mockingly.

"Ladies, please take your seats the auction will resume in five minutes." The M.C. announced to the crowd.

"Here you go ma'am." The waitress handed me my drink. "Is there anything else I can get for you?"

"Just keep'em coming." I relished the taste of the drink.

"Uh oh, look." Dylan pointed her head towards the door. "Here comes the mafia."

Suddenly my heart dropped down to my knees and my drink slipped through my fingers. Red tomato juice and vodka was all over my white ensemble. But that was the least of my worries. The fact that I was 30 years old and the mere mention of Isabel Cartwright and her minions Annabelle and Mirabel caused me to drop my drink worried me more. I hadn't seen The Mafia in ten years. Nothing about them had changed.

They still commanded the attention of everyone when they entered the room. Isabel was the leader of the pack and my sworn enemy since the first grade. Isabel was everything I wasn't. She was posed, elegant, calculating, manipulative and cunning. On the surface she was perfect. Not a strand on her pretty little head was ever out of place. I hated to admit it but Isabel was still breathtakingly gorgeous. Long dark tresses cascaded down her back. Her skin was a clear shade of butter. She was 5'10; model thin with cheekbones that could cut a bitch and possessed a wickedly beautiful smile. Seeing her look so well made me despise her even more.

Since as far back as I could remember Isabel and the rest of the Cashmere Mafia always wore cashmere cardigans hence them being called the Cashmere Mafia. Isabel and her crew were an elite group of bitches whose name all ended in Belle. Throughout grade school, junior high and even high school everyone feared them even me. I especially feared Isabel. For whatever reason she'd made it her life's mission to make my life a living hell. As if me being overweight with sever facial acne wasn't enough.

Isabel never bothered Dylan because everyone loved Dylan. She gave me and Tee-Tee the blues though. In grade school she use to pull my hair, take my lunch, push me, make everyone give me the silent treatment and excluded me from all birthday and slumber parties.

In gym I was always picked last and no one ever sat with me at lunch. She taunted me constantly about my acne and the fact that I had a double chin and a fat belly. No one except Tee-Tee, Dylan, Damon and my girl Emma Jean dared to be my friend. Well Tee-Tee and Dylan didn't have a choice. Everyone else feared the wrath of Isabel. She could turn you into a social outcast with one snap of the finger. By the time we reached high school she'd dubbed me Piggy. No matter how much I protested the name stuck.

Imagine walking through the halls at school and hearing your classmates snort and snicker as you walk by. I absolutely hated going to school and it was all because of the Cashmere Mafia. But I had something Isabel wanted, which was Damon. From the time we were in diapers it was well know that Damon and I would be married. His mother and my mother were best friends.

He and I grew up right next door to one another and were best friends. We didn't actually begin to date until high school. My acne had cleared and I'd lost fifteen pounds but was still considered fat. I honestly didn't know what Damon saw in me. I was overweight, shy, quiet and meek. Despite all of my flaws, Damon saw beauty in me. It wasn't until he and I started to date that the teasing died down some. Isabel still got her digs in whenever she could.

Like Isabel, Damon was popular. He was handsome as hell, smart and the captain of the football team. He even played Lacrosse. He could've had any girl he wanted but he chose me. When he chose me Isabel lost her god forsaken mind. Her hatred towards me magnified. She spread rumors that I smelled like fish, that I had crabs and that I was adopted.

The rumor that I was adopted, I almost believed myself. I mean you see how my mother treats me. Between her and Isabel I didn't know who hated me more. Every summer up until I was seventeen my mother shipped me off to fat camp. Thankfully despite the Mafia's constant ridicule of me, Damon's feelings for me never waivered.

Damon loving me despite my insecurities and the Belle's bullying made me love him to the moon and back.

Damon was my everything. He was my first love, my first sex partner and the first man I believed would never hurt me. When he and I were together I felt beautiful. He always made me feel safe. Damon and I would talk about how our life would be once we graduated from high school and college. We discussed how we would raise our children while balancing our careers. We had the perfect life planned out for ourselves. Our relationship was nothing short of a fairytale. But like all fairytales the evil witch always strikes and wreaks havoc.

I wasn't even all the way through my sophomore year of college when my world came crashing down. Word spread around campus that Isabel was pregnant. I didn't think anything of it because Isabel was known to sleep around. But when Tee-Tee told me that the rumor was that Damon was the father, my whole entire existence was wiped away. I will never forget the day I confronted Damon. He and I sat on my dorm room bed.

"Did you sleep with Isabel?" I asked, with clammy hands.

Damon glared off into the distance with a look of sorrow written all over his face. He couldn't even answer me. The tears that slipped from his eyes revealed all. Up until that moment Damon had been my savior. He made me feel like the love he had for me was real. But deep down inside I knew that I guy like him could never really love a girl like me. My acne had cleared but I was still pudgy Sunday Rose with no backbone.

He begged and begged for my forgiveness but there was no way I could give it to him. If he and Isabel had been a one time thing maybe just maybe I could've found room in my heart for forgiveness. But he and Isabel had been sleeping together since our senior year of high school. Apparently the only reason Isabel didn't spill the beans was because Damon threatened that if she told, he'd cut her off for good. Isabel figured that if she became pregnant by him that he would be forced to not keep her a secret.

Isabel's planned work. She had finally demolished me. I'd had enough. Before anyone could stop me, I dropped out of college and was on the first flight to L.A. I never turned back once but now here I was ten years later with tomato juice all over my outfit and a rapidly beating heart. It was like Isabel could smell my fear. Her spider senses located me and we caught eyes. She and her two minions made a beeline in my direction.

"Dylan, darling, how are you?" She air-kissed both of her cheeks.

"Isabel." Dylan politely spoke back.

"You look fabulous as always." She examined Dylan's outfit. "Seth." Isabel shot my brother an evil glare.

"Hooker." Tee-Tee shot back rolling his eyes.

"Well-well-well look who we have here," Isabel smirked looking down on me. "Still clumsy I see, Piggy."

"And you're still a bitch I see," I sneered, wiping the stain off of my top. "And my name ain't no damn Piggy."

"Looks like living out in the big city has given someone a potty mouth and a bad case of dry skin," Isabel quipped.

I so wanted to hit her with a snappy comeback but there was no denying it. I looked liked LeBron James scrotum. *Why in the hell did this bitch have to catch me on my off day?*

"Is there something you want Isabel 'cause the auction is about to resume and nobody has time for you and your high school shenanigans. We are not kids anymore and I am not here for your bullshit." I warned, feeling my temperature rise.

"Reer!" Isabel hissed, putting up her claws. "Piggy, calm down. I just came over to welcome you home." She leaned down to hug me.

"And to tell you…" She spoke low enough that only I could hear her words. "to stay the fuck away from husband."

Like the Stepford wife she was Isabel stood up straight with a gigantic fake smile on her face.

"You ladies and gentleman," she looked down at Tee-Tee. "enjoy the auction," she waved, walking away.

"What that heffa say to you?" Tee-Tee leaned over and whispered. "'Cause I am TTG, trained to muthafuckin' go!" He picked up his knife.

51

"Nothing worth repeating. Let me go to the bathroom and get cleaned up." I rose from my seat not realizing that what I thought was a napkin was actually the table cloth.

Before I could stop it from happening, I pulled the entire table cloth and everything on top of it on the floor. Glasses, plates, forks, spoons and the entire floral arrangement came crashing down. Dylan and Tee-Tee tried to scoot away but they were too late. Their drinks had spilled all over them. *That did not just happen*, I thought. But it had and all eyes were on me. My mother hung her head in shame. The Mafia laughed and pointed at me. Mrs. Mary Beth fainted and the rest of the Pink Hats shook their heads and whispered amongst themselves about me. *I swear to god this is all North West fault.*

Gotta bitch... what you want me for?

-Chris feat AV, "Cut Up"

Chapter 4

I tried my hardest to erase the memory of me making a complete ass out of myself at the Pink Hat's auction but the memory kept haunting me. I hadn't even been home two weeks and already I was back to being made fun of. After years of revamping my image and turning myself into the no nonsense diva I am now, no one seemed to care. Around here I was still Piggy. I thought that I would come home and people would see the new me and treat me with respect but I guess nothing about me had changed at all.

I maybe considered pretty and lost all of my weight but in my home town I still felt small and insignificant. I still had time to prove myself to be more than a klutz and a drunk which I'm not. In a few weeks my business would be open and I'd be setting up lonely souls all over the Midwest. Hell, somebody has to find love even if I haven't found my true love yet.

My date with Blue was a total waste of time. He was cute and somewhat intriguing but I've dated more than my share of industry cats back in L.A. Every time I ended up with a broken heart and a pillowcase full of tears. Fuck that, I am not about to go down that road again. My next date was coming up soon. According to my brother in-law Bernard he had my future husband on lock. I wasn't about to get my hopes up, though.

Nope, I'm going to focus all of my attention on making sure that my new *Two Hearts* location is perfect. 702 played softly while I unwrapped paintings for the office. I wanted my second location to have a modern monochromatic feel to it. The walls were painted stark white. All of the furniture is black. My office has an art gallery vibe that I love. I was thoroughly enjoying my time alone vibing out to Meelah from 702's airy voice when my whole afternoon was fucked up.

As I stood on a small ladder, I heard the sound of someone knocking on the door. I glanced over my shoulder to see who it was. When I connected eyes with the unexpected visitor, I almost dropped the painting I was hanging. Damon was at the door. See this is the shit I don't have time for. Thoroughly heated, I stepped down off the ladder and placed the painting on the floor. I kept the hammer in my hand just in case I needed to use it.

"What is it?" I asked, through the door.

"You gon' let me in?" He asked, looking like the sexiest man on the planet.

See this is some bullshit. How dare he show up at my place of business looking all good and shit. Every time I'm in this man's presence I lose all sense of myself. It's not fair that the older Damon gets the finer he looks. I mean, damn this shit has got to be illegal. Damon stood on the opposite side of the door looking like he'd stepped out of a Dolce & Gabbana ad campaign. Everything about him was mesmerizing.

Damn is 6 feet tall with skin the color of sweet caramel. He donned a low cut that was always impeccably lined. His smoldering brown eyes, smooth beard and succulent full lips drew me into him every time. Damon had one huge tattoo of an eagle that draped over his left shoulder and across his back. After years of playing high school and college football his body was ripped with muscles.

His body had been perfectly crafted by god. He and Omari Hardwick could've been twins. That afternoon he wore a Dolce & Gabbana, charcoal martini stretch-wool suit, with a crisp white button up and Salvatore Ferragamo caesy brogue oxford shoes. It was after 5 o' clock so he'd just gotten off work. Like myself, Damon comes from a very influential family. His family owned half of the casino's in St. Louis. Damon was now a principal owner in the family business.

Lord, I can't deal with this right now, I thought unlocking the door. Damon stepped over the threshold and the smell of his Creed Spice and Wood cologne enveloped me. Why does this man do this to me? Why did I have to once again look like a bum? My hair was up in a ponytail. I wore a pair of gold bamboo earrings, a gray cut off sweatshirt, black leggings and Tims.

"Welcome home baby girl." He hugged me tight.

I hated how all of my confidence was swept away when near him. Being in his arms again morphed me back to a time when I was his and he was mine. But he wasn't mine. Damon belonged to someone else.

"What are you doing here? How did you even know I was here and who told you where my office was at?" I said at once. Reluctantly I released myself from his embrace.

"Which question would you like for me to answer first?" Damon folded his arms across his chest.

His eyes were roaming all over my toned stomach and round hips.

"You know what? Never mind." I waved him off. "I already know who told you."

I'ma kick Tee-Tee's ass.

"You look beautiful," he replied, honestly.

"No, I don't. I look like shit but thank you."

"Nice place." He bypassed me and looked around.

My new office was nice but quaint. There was just enough room for me and the two assistants that I had yet to hire.

"Thank you. Now what do you want, Damon?" I asked, willing myself not to lose my shit.

"I came to see you." He turned and faced me. "You know it's pretty messed up that I had to find out you were back in town from my brother. You weren't going to call and tell me yourself?"

This nigga is crazy. He really thinks that I owe him something. Well, if he thinks he's going to get an explanation out of me, he's got another thing coming. I ain't telling his ass shit! Instead of answering him, I shot him a nasty look and tightened my grip around the hammer.

"So I take it you're still mad at me?" He inched closer.

I still didn't respond but my insides quivered with each step he took.

"How many times do I have to tell you, I'm sorry? I never meant to hurt you."

"Look, what do you want Damon? As you can see, I'm busy." I felt my temperature rise.

"Now that you're back home for good. I want us to be ok. We're going to run into each other so…" He ran his index finger slowly down the side of my face.

"Don't touch me." I smacked his hand away. "Don't ever touch me again." I snapped, walking past him.

"C'mon Sunday." Damon reached out and grabbed me by the hand. "This has to stop. You know I love you."

"Fuck you!" I yelled, slapping his face.

I hit him so hard that the imprint of my hand immediately popped up on his skin.

"You don't know shit about love!" My voice cracked.

"You know I've loved you since we were kids," he stressed.

"Sure you love me. You loved me enough to cheat on me and get that bitch pregnant! Then on top of that you fuckin' married the bitch had another kid with her! Those six years that I didn't speak to you were the best years of my life. I don't know what possessed me to let you in that night but I have regretted my decision ever since!" My bottom lip trembled.

I was trying my best to hurt him and by the look on his face it was working. But I was only being honest. After

I left St. Louis and moved to L.A. I put Damon, Isabel, my mother and everyone else who had made my life a living hell behind me. I found myself in L.A. I found my voice, my swag and my sense of style. I had a booming business. My life was on course. I was doing great until one fateful night my doorbell rang. I'd been in L.A. for six years at the time.

Damon McKnight had become a figment of my imagination. I never spoke his name. That was until; I opened my door to find him standing there. Stunned weren't even the words to describe how I felt. To this day I'm surprised I didn't faint. I had no idea why he was there. He didn't even utter a word to give an explanation.

He simply took me into his arms and kissed me passionately. That night we made love until the following afternoon. It was one of the best and worst nights of my life because little did I know that for the next three years I would become Damon McKnight's mistress. Whenever he visited L.A. he stayed with me. When he took business trips, I'd accompany him. We took vacations together and we spoke on the phone everyday we were apart.

I'd allowed myself to fall for him again. He swore that he was going to leave Isabel. But after three years and excuse after excuse I got tired of waiting on Damon to live up to his promise so I cut him off. I ex'd him completely out of my life as I'd done before. It'd been a full year since we last spoke. Now here he was trying to drag me down the rabbit hole once more.

"For three years," I got up in his face and mushed him in the forehead. "I let yo' tired ass string me along and make me believe that you were going to leave her! And like a dummy I waited! I put my life on hold for you," I cried, uncontrollably.

"Now look at me!" I threw my hands up in the air. "I'm 30 years old with no husband and no family! You stole my life from me not once but twice!" I emphasized the point with my fingers.

This is some bullshit! Why the fuck am I letting let this nigga make me cry? I'ma G and G's don't cry. Fuck his big head ass. He doesn't deserve me or my tears.

"Let me tell you something." He backed me up into a corner.

Oh shit, I thought.

"I'ma let you get that shit off but don't ever put your hands on me again," Damon warned.

"I don't even know why we're having this conversation right now. You're married!"

"You know I don't love her."

"I can't do this with you again." I pushed him out of my way.

"I have come too far to turn back now. I'm nobody's side chick. I spent three years fantasizing about the possibility of us being together and for what? All you did was make excuse after excuse as to why you couldn't leave yet. I mean, thank god that none of my family knew! I was raised better than that! Look," I composed myself. "I don't wanna have nothing to do wit' you."

"Isabel and I are separated. We're getting a divorce."

"Good for you," I spat, trying to pretend like I didn't care.

"I'm serious."

Damon wouldn't lie about something so serious so I knew he was telling the truth. The thing is why did I care if he was telling the truth or not? So what if he was leaving Isabel. I was not about to play the fool for him again.

"Damon, just do us both a favor and leave." I sighed, over it.

"Sunday, I told you it was complicated. All I needed was a little more time but you flipped off the handle like you always do and just cut me off."

"You damn right, I did. It's been a year since we last spoke Damon and from the ring on your finger it looks like you're still married. You have had all the time you needed to leave her ass if you wanted to. Oh and while we're on the subject of your wack ass marriage. Your stank ass wife just warned me last week to stay away from you so I suggest you leave."

"Fuck her! She's jealous of you. She always has been." He swung his arm, frustrated.

"Oh my god. I am so over this tired ass conversation." I shrilled, running my hands over the top of my head. "Will you just leave?"

"No and yo' ass damn for sure ain't gon' make me."
Damon ice grilled me.

"Whatever." I stomped my way back up the ladder.

"What are you doing?"

"Hanging a picture. What does it look like?" I
quipped.

"Move, man." Damon took off his suit jacket and
threw it on the floor.

His pecks and biceps showed through his shirt.
Lord, what did I do wrong to deserve this?

"I don't need your help," I snapped.

"You are so freakin' hard headed." Damon placed
his hands underneath my arms, lifted me off the ladder and
sat me down on the floor. "Give me the hammer. You don't
know what you're doing."

I didn't want to but I groaned and handed him the
hammer.

"So what's this nonsense I hear about you asking your family to set you up on dates in order for you to find a husband?" Damon hammered a nail into the wall.

"I swear to god Tee-Tee talks too damn much." I rolled my eyes, standing back on one leg.

"Don't you think that sounds a little ridiculous?" Damon asked over his shoulder.

"No... I don't."

"I'm not down for this lil' game you're playing." Damon hung the picture on the wall and got down off the ladder.

Standing before me he gazed into my eyes and said, "You're not going out on any fuckin' dates. You're mine and I'm yours and can't nobody change that. Not Isabel or any of these lame ass dudes you call yourself trying to go out wit'."

"Who in the hell do you think you're talking to?" I rolled my neck.

"I'm talking to you, Sunday. You! Everyday of my life I think about you, what you're doing or who you're wit'. Can't you see? I don't want nobody else but you. I tried to get over you. I tried to pray you away but you're here." He pointed to his chest where his heart was located.

"You understand that? You're it for me. You!" He pulled out his wallet and opened it up.

"Even when you're not with me, you're with me." Damon shoved a picture of me in my face. "You and my kids are all that I care about."

There it was, a picture of me. Right next to the picture of me was a picture of his two daughters. The sight of his girls killed me. I was supposed to be the mother of his kids.

"Your girls are beautiful." My eyes welled up with tears.

"Stop crying. You know I hate to see you cry." Damon wiped my tears away.

"I can't do this again." I allowed myself to cry.

"Shhhhh." He silenced me with a kiss.

"Damon we can't." I put up a feeble protest.

"Sunday shut up. I'm done talkin'. My dick is hard."

On everything I love tried so hard not to fall for the okie doke but my body had a mind all it's on. How could I say no to him? For as long as I can remember he's been my reason for living. Damon was home. He was the answer to everything fucked up in my life. If we could just fix this shit and make it right, we'd be ok. I'd be ok. There would be no more lonely nights. I wouldn't have to pray to God to send me my husband. Deep down inside, I knew I'd already found him.

But Damon was a married man. I was his mistress. I swore to myself that I'd never go back. I thought I'd closed the door on us but here I was being lifted up onto his shoulders so that my pussy lips could meet with his hungry tongue. I looked into his eyes.

"I love you." He mouthed before burying his face between my thighs.

I know this shit isn't right. I'm setting myself up for failure like always. I can't keep telling myself that loving him is ok. I love him and he loves me but he also loves her. I deserved my house with the white picket fence, two children and a dog. Damon promised me that and more but how long was I supposed to wait?

It just sucks that no other man has been able to capture my heart like him. It didn't help either that Damon's tongue stroke my clit with velvet ease. Each lick took me to Italy, Japan and Rome. For so long, I'd fooled myself into believing that I was over him. But after all this time I still cared. I hated that I did, though. He'd chosen her over me. How could I ever forgive him?

I couldn't but the hold he had on me since we were kids was still there. My head was filled with so many thoughts that the room was beginning to spin. Each flick of Damon's tongue caused my stomach to contract. There was no way I could hold on any longer.

"Tell me you love me," Damon ordered.

For a brief second we just stared at one another. My throat filled with tears. If only he knew how every beat of my heart yearned for him. I more than loved him. I needed him like I needed air to breathe. Time stands still whenever he is near. When he's not around I don't know how to function. Damon McKnight was it for me. He was my one and only true love.

"I love you…"

Friends may come and friends may go.

-Brandy, "Best Friend"

Chapter 5

What the fuck is wrong with me? It's like I get off on self torture. I had no business sleeping with Damon, although the dick was extraordinary. I mean good god almighty it was sinfully delicious. That man knows exactly how to rock my pussy to sleep but fuck that! No, Sunday! You have to keep reminding yourself that he's the enemy.

Damon is a bad guy. He doesn't mean you any good. Fucking with him is going to ruin you. Sleeping with him was a one time thing. You can not let that shit happen again. From this day forward I'm going to pretend like it never happened. Besides, I have bigger to fish to fry. I had amends to make.

My stomach was in knots as I pulled into Emma's driveway. Her home was beautiful. It looked like a house you'd see on Leave It To Beaver. Emma had her dream home. It was a colonial, country designed home. It was white with a blue roof and blue shutters around the windows. The lawn was perfectly manicured. She had a curved walkway with flowers strategically placed along side. A red Little Tike's car lay on its side in the grass next to a tricycle and other children's toys.

I just prayed that she'd be willing to see me. Nervously, I turned off the engine and got out of the car. My palms were sweaty as hell as I approached her door. I hadn't spoken to Emma in nine years. When I left St. Louis I swore to her that we'd talk everyday and that I'd write. For a year I did but after a while, I ended up spending more time with my new friends. When Emma called I found myself too busy to answer or I'd tell her I'd call her back and never would.

Soon all communication stopped and like everybody else in my life Emma became a figment of my past. While in L.A. I often thought about her but so much time had past. I felt awkward trying to pick up the phone to call. But now that I was back home I had no choice but to face my fears and past transgressions. Emma deserved better from me and as a I friend I'd let her down. If I did nothing else in life I had to make things right with Emma.

Inhaling deep, I swallowed hard and knocked. I could hear a baby crying hysterically and loud classical music playing.

"The door is open!" Emma shouted over the noise.

Confused as to why she'd be letting random people in her house, I twisted the knob and walked in. My forehead immediately scrunched at the sight of Emma's home. There was shit everywhere. It looked like Babies R Us had farted all over her living room. There were toys, two playpens, baby shoes, juice cups, bottle and blankets all over the furniture and floor. Emma's oldest son and my godson Jackson sat directly in front of the flat screen playing the Xbox. Jackson had a set of head phones with a microphone attached to it on. He was talking major trash and had no clue that I had walked inside.

"You can't see me dog! You don't want none of me cuz!" He said to whoever was on the other end.

I don't even know how he could concentrate with all of the noise surrounding him. His three year old brother Jacob was in his playpen crying at the top of his lungs. Tears strolled down his chubby cheeks and snot ran from his nose. His screams were making my lady parts hurts.

"Mommy's coming Jacob!" Emma yelled from the kitchen.

Jacob's shrills along with the classical music were driving me insane. I had to do something.

"Come here man." I reached inside the playpen and picked him up. "Who made you mad, huh?" I bounced him up and down.

Jacob instantly stopped crying.

"You know you're too cute to be making so much noise." I walked over to the stereo and turned the volume down.

Jackson noticed and swiftly took his headphones off.

"Mom! There's some crazy black lady in our house holding Jacob?" He scooted back in a panic.

"What?!" Emma ran into the living room with her six month old daughter draped in one of those African baby slings.

As soon as she spotted me she stopped dead in her tracks.

75

"Jackson this crazy lady is your godmother, Sunday Rose." Emma's chest heaved up and down.

"Word? I thought she was a mythical creature you came up with but what up G Ma." Jackson shot me a head nod and resumed playing the game.

"How in the hell did you get in my house?" Emma asked, clearly not happy to see me.

"Hi Emma," I waved awkwardly.

Emma had grown into a stunning woman. The last time I saw her we were twenty and she was going through her grunge faze. Emma was now the poster child for suburban moms. Her hair was back to her natural shade of chestnut brown. She wore it long now with loose waves. Her porcelain skin was lily white. Homegirl, was in desperate need of a spray tan. Like myself, Emma had doe shaped blue eyes but something about her was different.

She hadn't grown any. She was still 5'5 with a dimpled chin, plump lips, B Cup boobs and a small waist. What in the hell about her has changed? Maybe it was the fact that she looked like a stay-at-home-mom. Emma wore a white v-neck long sleeve fitted shirt, yoga pants and tan

Ugg boots. But that still wasn't it. Holy shit! Emma got a nose job. Her once crooked pug nose was now pointy and straight.

"You finally did it," I smiled, examining her face. "You gotta freakin' nose job. Good for you, Emma Jean."

"Will you hush?" Emma spoke sternly. "My kids don't know that mommy hasn't always had this nose."

"Why not? You look amazeballs."

"Once again how did you get into my house Single Black Female?" She mean-mugged me.

"I knocked and you told me to come in." I ran my hand through Jacob's curly blonde hair.

"Oh." She looked me up and down. "I thought you were the cable guy. What are you doing here, though?" Emma turned her back on me and went back into the kitchen.

"I'm here because I've moved back in town and I wanted to see you." I followed her.

Emma's kitchen was huge. Unlike the outside of the house her kitchen was very modern. All of the appliances were stainless steel. In the center of the room was a built-in island with a table top oven and sink. She had hardwood floors and lots of lighting. Despite all the mess Emma's house was pretty dope.

"Sunday, we haven't spoken in nine years. Let's keep it that way ok and put my son down." Emma put her daughter inside her pumpkin seat.

"Did you not hear him in there screaming? This child clearly needs a hug or better yet some Benadryl." I looked at Jacob and smiled.

He smiled back.

"As you can see I only have two hands. I can't fix a bottle and make the boys lunch at the same time," Emma replied, clearly flustered.

Seeing Emma so stressed out I put Jacob in his high chair.

"Let me help you. You finish making..." I stopped and pondered. "What's her name?" I referred to her baby girl.

"Jada!" Emma gave me the evil eye. "My daughter's name is Jada."

"You always did have a weird obsession with Jada Pinkett." I went into the cabinet and pulled out a box of Cheerios.

"She's the greatest actress on earth. I don't know why she hasn't won an Academy Award yet," Emma said, seriously.

"Sure, her performance in The Matrix was legendary," I mocked her. "Where's your bread? I'll make the boys a sandwich."

"You are fucking insane." Emma eyed me in disbelief.

"Mom! You have to put a dollar in the swear jar!" Jackson shouted from the living room.

"Shit!" Emma bit into her bottom lip.

"I heard that!" Jackson laughed.

"Shut up Jackson! Now back to you. What makes you think that you can just give me your ass to kiss for nine years and then just show up as if nothing has happened?

You haven't picked up the phone and called me in nine years. Hell, you haven't even checked on your so called godson. Do you even know how old Jackson is now?"

"I don't know, like 25... 30," I shrugged.

"He's eight." Emma's face turned bright red.

"Close enough. I send him a birthday gift every year," I replied, taking out a pack of Oscar Meyer bologna, Hellmann's mayonnaise and Kraft American cheese.

"You send him the same gift every year Sunday; a Superman onesie and a remote control car!" Emma shot back.

"No, the real question is why the hell are you still eating Hellmann's?" I ignored her sarcasm.

"Didn't we have a discussion when we were ten that Miracle Whip is better? This shit is disgusting. I know it's a white folks thing but this here looks like geez." I pretended to throw up.

"This is not a joke, Sunday. You can't joke your way out of this. I'm not playing with you. We're no longer friends. You made sure of that."

"I know," I said, seriously. "It's all my fault. I'm sorry Emma. I'ma piece of shit. I never thought that when I moved to L.A. that you and I would grow apart. We use to do everything together."

"We didn't grow apart. You pushed me to the side for your Hollywood friends." She put up air quotes. "You left me here by myself with these vultures. I had nobody but John."

"What about Tee-Tee?"

"Well yeah but he cusses me out every five seconds about my hair and my clothes and the fact that I don't wear any makeup. I love him to death but Tee-Tee can be quite a bit much at times. I needed you Sunday. You were supposed to be my best friend," Emma stressed.

"I am your best friend. I just got caught up in my own hype. I thought about you all the time."

"Then why didn't you call?" Emma countered.

"So much time passed by that I didn't think you would want to talk to me," I answered truthfully.

"You were right about that," Emma said with a laugh.

"Emma." I reached across the kitchen island and took her hand. "I'm genuinely sorry. I really mean it. If you let me, I promise to be the best friend you've ever had. I'll bring you chocolate chip cookies, cupcakes and we'll watch movies together all the time. Hell, I'll even babysit your bad ass kids."

"Now that I'll take you up on," Emma giggled.

"I love you friend."

"I love you too," Emma groaned, rolling her eyes to the ceiling.

"Now explain to me why your house looks like the Tasmanian devil ran through it?" I questioned concerned.

"After taking care of the kids, cooking, having play dates and soccer practice; by the end of the day I'm exhausted. There is simply not enough time in the day for me to do everything. It's hard, Sunday. Sometimes I feel like I'm having a nervous breakdown," Emma replied with tears in her eyes.

"Why doesn't John help?"

"He's at work all day and when he comes home he's tired too."

"Well honey you need to A) get Jackson's ass off of that damn game and up cleaning. He's old enough to help. You also need to hire a maid and possibly a nanny. Ain't nothing wrong with a little help," I remarked.

"I'm not letting some young hot chick in my house when I walk around all day looking like this." Emma looked down at her outfit.

"We'll make sure she's elderly with several missing teeth and a mustache. How about that?" I joked.

"I like the sound of that. Thank god you're home. Are you coming to our high school reunion next week?"

"What reunion?" I asked confused.

"Umm it's our ten year reunion this year. Tee-Tee or Dylan didn't tell you?"

"No." I shook my head.

"Well, it's literally next weekend."

"Why are they having our reunion in the dead of winter?" I asked.

"It's Isabel's idea. She wanted to have a winter wonderland ball. As you know what Isabel wants, Isabel gets." Emma played with Jada's tiny little feet.

"Lord," I sighed.

"So it'll be a one night thing. We're having a formal banquet dinner and dance next Saturday," Emma explained.

"Mmm."

"I heard about what happened to you at the Pink Hats auction," Emma snickered.

"So you knew I was back in town?" I threw a piece of bread at her head.

Emma dodged the throw and laughed.

"I know everything that happens in this god forsaken town. Being a stay-at-home-mom isn't so bad. You learn all the tea, girl."

"So what's the tea on Isabel and Damon?" I probed putting both ends of the sandwiches together.

84

"Why do you wanna know?" Emma asked not missing a beat.

"'Cause I do, Emma," I declared, bucking my eyes.

"Well Isabel likes to pretend that they're in wedded bliss but from what I hear," Emma looked around the room to make sure no one else could hear. "they're separated. Megan's husband and Damon hoop together and he told Meagan that Damon told him that they don't even sleep in the same room anymore."

Wow so he was telling the truth.

"That's interesting." I tried my hardest not to smile.

"Yeah, it looks like Isabel's fictional fairytale is coming to an end. So are you coming to the reunion?"

"I don't know," I shrugged. "It's last minute. I don't have a date. I don't wanna come by myself looking like a loser."

"You can come with John and me," Emma offered.

"That's sweet Emma but no. I'll figure something out. Have you found a dress?" I asked cutting the sandwiches in two.

85

"Yeah, it's just a simple black dress, nothing fancy."

"Oh honey no," I shook my head. "There will be nothing simple about you at this reunion. We're going shopping."

I had you, I had it all.
-Alex Isley, "F.D.A."

Chapter 6

"Ok Sunday you can do this." I inhaled deep.

I'd been sitting outside the Four Season's hotel for thirty minutes. My high school reunion Winter Wonderland Ball was in full swing but I was too afraid to go in. When I moved back to St. Louis, I had all of the confidence in the world but after the fiasco at the Pink Hats auction, I felt myself morph back to the awkward adolescent I used to be. But I couldn't let one unfortunate incident ruin me. I've changed. I'm no longer the fat, soft spoken girl whom everybody called Piggy.

No, I'm Sunday Rose Vasi. I'm sexy. I'm confident. I'm successful and I can read a bitch for filth if need be. Besides, I'm about to kill these hoes in the worst way. Everything about me that night was on point. My body was lathered in gold shimmer lotion. I was serving sweet cunt fish in a metallic Jason Wu dress.

The sequin-embroidered chiffon slinky dress had a halter neck with low-cut cutaway shoulders and a draped bare back. The partial sheer hem of the dress stopped right above my ankles. My tits were sitting up honey with no bra. I was going to serve these broads toned back, ample bosom and a round ass. The only undergarments I could wear underneath the dress was a tiny nude g-string.

"C'mon girl, lets do this." I picked up my fabulous hand-poured clear confetti acrylic Edie Parker clutch from the passenger seat and got out.

It was cold as hell but my waist length chinchilla fur kept me warm. My 4 inch stiletto, mirrored ankle strap, Gianvito Rossi sandals clicked across the pavement as I made my way inside. Once I got to the banquet hall, I was greeted by Catalina Vasquez. In high school Catalina was a know-it-all Mexican girl that worked my nerves. From the looks of her time hadn't been on Catalina's side. Nothing about her screamed twenty-nine. She looked at least 45 years old.

"OMG," she gasped. "Piggy?! Is that you?" She stood from her chair.

Don't cuss her out Sunday. Don't cuss her out.

"It's Sunday, Catalina." I replied in an even tone.

"Oh, I'm sorry." She slapped her hand against her forehead.

"Old habits die hard. You look phenomenal. I heard that you were in L.A. doing well but my gosh." She looked me up and down in awe. "You are doing it girl. What did you do? Did you get the lap band 'cause I've been considering it?"

"No, I changed my diet and started to exercise."

"Oh," Catalina replied, disappointed by my response. "Let me get your name tag." She looked around the table.

"Here you go." She handed me mine.

To my dismay my name tag had Piggy written on it.

"Is there anyway you can give me another one. This one has Piggy written on it." I tried handing it back to her.

"Noooooo, unfortunately I don't have anymore." Catalina smirked, sitting back down.

Oh so this bitch is trying me. I got her ass. With a smile on my face, I proudly put the name tag on my chest.

"Listen," I leaned forward and got into her face. "Just because you look like the Mexican version of Ms. Trunchbull doesn't mean that you have to be a bitter silly bitch. Get it together, Catalina. Enjoy the ball," I smiled, brightly.

Pleased with myself I sauntered into the banquet hall. The room was decorated gorgeously. It was so pretty it almost resembled a wedding reception. Blue up-lights shined on the ceiling. All of the tables were draped with crisp white linens, white china, white flower petals and crystals. Each table had huge white trees on them. There were candles everywhere.

Isabel had outdone herself as always. I swear there was nothing this chick couldn't do. Everyone from our class was there looking classy and sophisticated in their gowns and tuxedos. It was weird to see everyone so grown up. Mostly, everyone looked the same. Some people had gained weight, lost weight, changed their hair, lost hair, or were pregnant. I searched the room for Emma Jean and spotted her and her husband talking to a group of people.

With my shoulders back, I walked confidently over to them.

"Sunday!" Emma exclaimed, running towards me.

She looked stunning. I had my hairstylist and makeup artist, Delicious give her the red carpet special. Emma was serving MILF realness in a pink Oscar de la Renta strapless ruffle-back bow gown.

"Honey, you are snatched" I snapped my fingers in approval.

"I know! John can't keep his hands off of me," she squealed.

"Uh oh somebody bout to get they back cracked tonight." I hugged her tight.

"You remember Chelsea, Derris and Cooper don't you?" She led me over to the group.

"Yes." I waved.

"This can't be Piggy," Derris said, shocked.

"It's me, Sunday," I corrected him.

"Damn girl, you fine as fuck. My wife needs to take a page outta your book." Derris licked his lips.

Derris was always such a perve.

"You look fantastic," Chelsea complimented me.

"Thank you."

"Have you seen Catalina and Beth Ann?" She whispered. "They are both as big as a house now."

"I saw Catalina." I replied, not liking the topic of conversation.

Sure, Catalina had been a bitch to me for no reason but I never liked when people made fun of other folks because of their weight. Being an ex fatty, I know all too well how name calling can destroy a person's self esteem.

"Thanks for making over my girl." John kissed Emma on the forehead. "We might be making baby number four tonight."

"Oh no the hell we aren't," Emma objected. "My baby making days are over. You are not about to use up all the rest of my good THOT years."

Emma had totally used the word THOT incorrectly but I didn't have the heart to tell her. She was glowing and seemed genuinely relaxed and happy.

"Oh lord, the Queen B has arrived." Cooper announced as Isabel made her entrance. "Let's all be on our best behavior or we'll feel the wrath of the Mafia."

"Good heavens Damon can sure fill out a suit." Chelsea clutched her pearls.

"He looks a'ight," I quipped.

"Oh, I forgot you two use to be an item," she laughed.

"Yeah, that was a long time ago," I replied, catching Damon's eye.

Chelsea was right, though. Damon looked succulent in his custom made Dsquared2 metallic micro-dot evening jacket. The lapel was black to match his black tuxedo shirt and pants. He and Isabel were the picture perfect couple. They were St. Louis very own JayZ and Beyoncé. My eyes followed him as he made his way around the room. Then he came my way. My heart began to race at a feverish pace. Damon was just too fine for words.

"How's everybody doing?" He spoke.

"Good." The group smiled.

"Sunday," He stared me square in the eyes.

"Damon," I responded, praying no one could see how hard my nipples were.

"Can I speak to you for a minute?" Damon placed his hand on the small of my back.

"Sure." I looked at Emma with a puzzled expression on my face.

Emma's round eyes widen.

"Don't go," she mouthed.

I felt bad for keeping my friend in the dark about Damon and I but no one could know about us. Damon and I stepped off to the side; far enough that no one could hear our conversation.

"What's up?" I said in a nonchalant tone.

"Why haven't you been answering any of my calls? I've been calling you all week." He spoke barely above a whisper.

"I've been busy."

"Bullshit." Damon stepped closer. "You gotta stop with this game you playing, Sunday."

"The only one who is playing a game is you," I remarked.

"I see you wore my favorite color." He slid his hand down the side my neck.

Did I just cum on myself? I think I did. Yep, I did. I can't even front. I wore the dress on purpose. Damon always loved to see me in metallic and I must admit I looked fabulous in it.

"You know what that shit do to me." His lips brushed up against my ear as he spoke.

I swallowed hard. This shit has got to stop.

"Can I come see you tonight?"

"You might wanna ask your wife that," I said, locking eyes with Isabel.

She was coming our way. From the tense look on her face I could tell she was pissed. She'd warned me to stay away from her husband and I wasn't abiding by her rules. I was being a bad little girl. Knowing Isabel I was sure to be punished for it. Little did she know but I was ready for war whenever or wherever.

"Baby." She intertwined her arm with Damon's. "What are you doing?"

"I was just saying hello to Sunday. We haven't seen each other in a long time."

"Let's keep it that way," Isabel said, sternly.

"Yo chill," Damon ice-grilled her.

"Excuse me?" Isabel drew her head back.

"You heard me," Damon advised.

"I'm about to head over to our table. I suggest you follow." Isabel shot us both a death glare and stormed off.

See this is the shit my grown ass doesn't have time for. Ain't nobody got time to be playing with Damon and Isabel.

"Can I come see you tonight?" Damon asked again as if nothing had happened.

"You need to go have a seat with your wife." I responded, visibly pissed.

Damon clenched his jaw tight. He hated when I played him like he was a chump.

"I know you ain't trippin' off that shit?" He asked genuinely shocked.

"I gotta to go." I walked away before he could stop me.

My brother and his husband had walked in. Thank god for them. I needed the distraction. I don't think anyone was prepared for Tee-Tee, though. My brother had made his grand entrance in a floor-length Emilio Pucci beaded lace & sheer panel gown. He almost looked better than me.

"Sissy that walk bitch!" I snapped my fingers in a Z formation.

"Yassss, I'm serving the kids and the faculty," Tee-Tee strutted across the room like Naomi Campbell. "These chicks ain't ready for the doll but P.S. do my arms look Michelle Obama toned or Madonna scary?"

"Michelle," I assured him.

"Whew" Tee-Tee wiped invisible sweat from his forehead. "Ok 'cause ya' girl was a little concerned."

"I told you," Bernard shook his head.

"Hi brother in-law," I hugged him. "Where are Dylan and Angel?"

"They had to stay at home. Mason has an ear infection," Bernard answered.

"Aww poor baby." I poked out my bottom lip. "I hope he feels better."

"We do too but what is up with this name tag, chile?" Tee-Tee scrunched up his forehead.

"You tell me. Ain't it some bullshit?" I rolled my neck.

"Oh no this will not do." Tee-Tee reached inside his purse for a pen.

He quickly ex'd out Piggy and wrote Sunday above it.

"There, much better," he smiled, pleased. "You betta let these bougie hoes know how the Vasi girls do."

"What would I do without you?" I pinched my brothers' cheek.

"Watch it heffa." He snatched his head back. "Don't mess up my makeup."

"Aww hush."

"But explain this to me. Why is Damon eye-fuckin' the hell outta you?" Tee-Tee glared across the room at him.

"I don't know. Don't pay him any attention." I waved him off.

For the next two hours we ate dinner, watched several performances and had an awards ceremony which was hosted by Annabelle and Mirabel. The award for class clown went to Andrew Rucker. Isabel nabbed best hair. I received the most improved award. Best smile went to LaKeisha Stallwell. LaKeisha switched up to the microphone with the same stank walk she had in high school.

"What's good? I wanna thank the number one OG in my world... the Lord. Wit' out him I wouldn't have this dope-ass smile. I wanna thank the streets that raised me and the 4500 block of Wren." She threw up the peace sign and went back to her seat.

A slow clap sounded off in the room. If LaKeisha Stallwell was raised in the hood I was raised by wolves. LaKeisha's parents were both surgeons and she lived a block over for me growing up.

"Okay," Annabelle cleared her throat. "Up next we have the award for biggest flirt and the winner is Seth Vasi," she sneered.

The Mafia hated Tee-Tee just as much as they despised me.

"My name is Teyana," Tee-Tee snatched the mic from her. "Aka Tee-Tee aka Beautiful Brown Bitch. I wanna thank Blue Ivy, North West and the entire Bey Hive 'cause without them none of this would be possible. Secondly, I want to thank my first boo, Jose. Jose taught me everything. He taught me how to back that thang up—"

"Okay that's enough!" Mirabel snatched the mic back from him.

"All praises to Coco Chanel" Tee-Tee yelled into the mic before being escorted back to his seat.

I stood from my seat and clapped so loud, I thought my hands were going to bleed. The Mafia was appalled by his speech but who cared.

"And our final award for the night is cutest couple. The winner of this award will share a spotlight dance. And most likely the cutest couple award goes to," Mirabel beamed, gleefully opening the envelope.

"Damon McKnight and Isa..." She stopped mid sentence. "This has to be a mistake." She turned and said to Annabelle.

Annabelle took the envelope from Mirabel's hand and looked down at the card. An angry expression was on her face.

"We're not sure if this is correct or not but the winner is Damon McKnight and Sunday Rose Vasi," Annabelle grimaced.

The entire room erupted in a thunderous applause. I was visibly stunned by the announcement. Never in a million years did I think Damon and I would get cutest couple. I mean, we had been high school sweethearts but everyone always thought Isabel was a better suit for him.

"Girl, you betta get up and go dance wit' yo' boo," Tee-Tee ushered me out of my seat.

I glanced nervously over at Emma. She was shaking her head as if to say don't go. Standing up, I walked towards the center of the dance floor. Damon arose from his seat and headed in the same direction. Everyone was cheering and whistling except for the Cashmere Mafia. Isabel looked like her head was about to explode. Annabelle and Mirabel stood by her side with their arms folded across their chest. If looks could kill I would've been dead.

This shit is crazy. I hated to be the center of attention. Yet, here I was on the dance floor with a huge spotlight beaming down on me. Damon stood before me. His eyes sparkled as he gazed into mine. Here we were once again being pulled together like two magnets. For the life of me why I can't I shake this nigga? He brings nothing but negativity into my life.

But when I'm near him I feel full. Damon didn't say a word. He took my hand in his and wrapped his other arm around my waist. KeKe's Wyatt's country themed song *Lie Under You* serenaded us as we danced. Behind us a

103

projector reflected old images on the wall of Damon and me. I was pretty sure that all eyes were on us but during that five minutes time stood still. It was only Damon and I in that room. Damon pressed his cheek up against mine and held me close.

"I'm moving out in a few weeks," he said.

I closed my eyes and pretended as if I hadn't heard him. But I had. I honestly didn't know how to respond so I continued to dance without uttering a response. Was I supposed to jump for joy because he was leaving his wife and kids? I didn't want him destroying his family for me.

"You and I are meant to be. Everyone can see it. Just give me the chance to prove it," he continued.

I swayed my hips to the beat and inhaled his intoxicating cologne. Maybe Damon and I were meant to be. He'd made a mistake. Maybe I should forgive him? But we'd been down this road before and he'd led me astray. I had to be smart this time. I couldn't let him trap me into some false sense of security. Isabel was his wife. I was his ex. It was best we kept it that way.

104

No matter how hard I tried I couldn't stop the tears that were building in my eyes. Knowing that Damon could've been mine and he wasn't was killing me inside. How I wish that I could erase the remnants of him from my heart. I couldn't though. He held a permanent place there. With tears in my eyes I opened them to find Emma staring directly at me. The look on her face was one I'll never forget. It was a mixture of disappointment and shock.

Emma knew me like the back of her hand. There would be no denying my feelings for Damon to her 'cause she knew our dirty little secret. It was written all over my face and his. I wondered who else could tell. Everyone else seemed unfazed by us except Isabel. Isabel looked like she'd been kicked in the stomach with a steel toe boot. Her worst nightmare was coming true. She thought after becoming pregnant with Damon's child she'd never see me in Damon's arms again.

Nothing could keep me and Damon apart. Not time, not distance, marriage or kids. I was his and he was mine. Isabel knew this. She wasn't going to give up Damon without a fight, though. She was going to make my life a living hell.

You bitches got me fucked up.

-Chris feat AV, "Cut Up"

Chapter 7

If there was one thing that I absolutely love; it was a good a spa day. I scheduled an appointment for myself at least twice a month. After the month I had back in St. Louis, I was in desperate need of a day filled with rest and relaxation. I was stressed the fucked out. My business still wasn't open. I hadn't found anyone suitable to work for me. I was paying rent on a space that was collecting dust by the day. I had to get my office doors open ASAP. Valentine's Day was only a few weeks away. There were people out there that needed my help. Somebody had to find true love even it wasn't me.

My sick infatuation with Damon wasn't helping either. Having him back in my life was driving me to drink. Now that Emma knew our secret it was just a matter of time before the rest of St. Louis knew too. But I couldn't think about that now. Today, I'm going to focus on absolutely nothing. Tee-Tee, Emma, Dylan and I were at the Four Seasons St. Louis Spa & Salon. I was thoroughly enjoying the urban oasis of tranquility.

The spa & salon held 12 luxuriously appointed treatment rooms, steam rooms, two whirlpools and a full service salon. After stripping down to my bra and panties I slipped into a nice comfy fluffy white robe and slippers. Ready to go we all locked our belongings in our lockers and walked out into the common area.

"So what would you all like to start off with first?" The attendant asked.

"I'm about that hot stone massage life, ya' feel me." Tee-Tee clicked his tongue.

"Me too." Dylan did the Cabbage Patch.

"Emma you wanna start off with a facial?" I asked.

"Sure," she agreed.

"We'll see ya'll in a minute." Dylan waved goodbye.

"Bye." I waved back.

"You ladies follow me this way." The attendant led us to our room which was breathtaking.

When I walked in, I felt as if I had been transported to a private island. The room was all white. The smell of lavender scented candles filled the room. Tranquil music serenaded us. Two perfectly made beds awaited us. Emma and I both got on our perspective beds and lie back.

"The facialists will be in just a second." The attendant spoke before leaving.

"Thank you," I said, crossing my legs.

"Thank you Jesus. Lord knows I needs this," Emma exhaled.

"Me too. I have been so stressed out lately. The opening of this second location is killing me. You know I'm starting to think that maybe I shouldn't have rushed things. Maybe I should've just taken some time off and collected myself. You know what?" I held my hand up to my face and examined my nails. "I think I'm going to get a mani/pedi too."

"You should get your eyebrows done too," Emma suggested.

109

"Is that a read bitch?" I held my head back.

"I'm just sayin," Emma laughed.

"Heffa please. My eyebrows are snatched tighter than Miguel's vagina," I quipped.

"Whatever. Ok, enough is enough. Cut the bullshit, Sunday," Emma remarked. "Every since the reunion you have been dancing around the big ass elephant in the room."

"I don't see no elephant in this room." I played dumb.

"Really Sunday?" Emma eyed me in disbelief.

"I seriously have no idea what you're talking about."

"Ok." She nodded her head. "I'ma play right along with you. If you wanna act like you don't know what I'm talking about then fine."

Annoyed, I flared my nostrils and let out a heavy sigh. I came to the spa to get away from my problems not discuss them. I was not in the mood to be called out on my bullshit. Everyday for the past four years I lived with my sins. Talking about them was only going to make them more real. Nope, I wasn't going to be sucked into Emma's guilt trip.

"Yep, we're going just to sit her and pretend like you're not sleeping with another woman's husband," Emma baited me. "And trust me; I can't stand Isabel just as much as you. But right is right and wrong is wrong and Sunday Rose Vasi yo' ass is as wrong as Mama Dee's leave out."

"He's leaving her." I couldn't help but say.

"Ain't that what they all say?" Emma looked at me like I was dumb.

"C'mon Sunday, you're smarter than this. Let alone you deserve better. Let's not forget what he did to you. If Damon loved you so much he would've never cheated on you in the first place." Emma spat as the facialists walked in.

I quickly shot her look to shut up. She did.

"Hello ladies. I'm Suzette and this is Janice." Suzette pointed to her co-worker.

"Hello." Emma and I spoke back.

"You ladies are both getting our Detoxifying-Vitamin facial, correct?"

"Yes," I replied.

"Ok, let's get started. First we're going to warm the skin and open your pores by placing a warm towel on your face."

"Ok," I replied, relishing the warm towel on my skin.

"We're going to let this sit for a few minutes and we'll be back. The door is open so we'll be right outside if you need anything." Suzette said as she and Janice left the room.

"Now back to you." I spoke once I was sure the facialists were all the way gone. "You're right. What Damon did to me was fucked up but we were young. He made a mistake. I have to forgive him at some point, right?"

"Yeah but that doesn't mean you have to fuck him," Emma retorted.

112

"That's a dollar in the swear jar, mommy." I mocked her.

"You don't take anything seriously, do you?"

"I take food and clothes very seriously," I laughed.

"Seriously, Sunday. I love you and I want nothing more than for you to be happy but Damon; he is not the one. So he said he's leaving her. How do you know for sure?" She asked, loudly.

"Can you talk a little quieter, please? I don't want everybody in St. Louis knowing my business." I hissed, feeling a breeze brush against my exposed skin.

"Just answer the question, home wrecker."

"He told me at the reunion that he's moving out," I answered.

"How long has this been going on?"

There was simply no way in hell that I was going to tell Emma the truth. She was already ripping my asshole a new one. Nope. I was going to lie-lie-lie.

"Since 2010," I admitted unable not to tell the truth.

"What?!" Emma screeched, jumping up.

"Will you shut up?!" I snatched the towel from my face.

"No you shut up!" Emma threw her towel at me.

I couldn't resist throwing mine back at her. It landed directly on the top of her head.

"You've been screwing him for 4 years?" She whispered, taking the towel off her head.

"Three... we took a year off." I looked the other way.

"You are such a dumb whore." Emma shook her head, displeased.

"There goes another dollar." I shot back.

"Alright ladies." Suzette and Janice reentered the room. "Let's get started on your facials. Will you both please lie back?"

Emma and I glared at each other and did as we were asked. By the look on her face, I knew she was beyond disappointed in me. Hell, I was disappointed in myself.

114

Maybe Emma was right. Maybe I was playing the role of the fool for Damon once again. He'd played me once before. Who's to say he won't do it again? However, this time with him seemed different. All of the things I'd asked of him before, he was now doing so why shouldn't I believe him?

I did have to look at the fact that Damon was married with children. I didn't want to be the one causing his kids any pain. Maybe I should wait until his divorce before I fully invested myself in him again. Yep, that's what I'ma do. There will be no more Damon McKnight for me. Only single available men will be worth my time.

"How does this feel?" Suzette asked placing the cream on face.

"It's really tingly. Is it supposed to feel that way?" I asked feeling uncomfortable.

"Umm a little bit," she responded.

"Mine feels great," Emma said.

"Why do I smell cucumber?" I sniffed the air. "Does this have cucumber in it 'cause it didn't say so on the brochure."

115

"No ma'am. There are no cucumbers in this." Suzette continued to lather the cream onto my face.

"Then why is my skin starting to itch?" I scratched my cheek. "The only thing that I'm allergic to is cucumber and I smell cucumber in this." I shot up, scratching my face profusely.

"I can assure you ma'am there is no cucumber extract in this cream," Suzette swore.

"Shit!" Janice cried out, jumping back.

"What?" I paused alarmed.

"Your face," she pointed frightened. "It's swelling up."

"Emma look at my face is it swollen?" I demanded with tears in my eyes.

"Friend, your face is as big as Kim K's ass." Emma's eyes grew wide.

I swiftly hopped off the table and ran over to the nearest mirror. Sure enough my face was swollen. I looked like Martin Lawrence on that episode of Martin where he got his ass kicked by Tommy "The Hit Man" Hearns.

"What in the Jennifer Love Hewitt is happening to my face?!" I shrieked.

The words hadn't even settled into the atmosphere when out of nowhere Isabel walked slowly past my door. She was dressed in a robe and slippers as well. I had no idea she was even at the spa. A gigantic wicked grin was plastered on her face as she arched her eyebrow and lifted a small bottle of cucumber extract from the pocket of her robe. Then it hit me.

The breeze I felt wasn't just a breeze that was Isabel sneaking out of our room. Everyone growing up knew that I was allergic to cucumber. At the country club they always served our water with a slice of cucumber and I couldn't have any. That heffa snuck into our room and placed cucumber extract into my facial crème. Isabel grinned and winked her eye at me. Homegirl was thoroughly pleased with herself. She'd fired the first shot. Now it was time for me to shoot back.

Can't keep yo' eyes off my fatty, daddy.

-Beyoncé feat Jay Z, "Drunk In Love"

Chapter 8

After being humiliated at the spa, the last thing I wanted to do was show my face anywhere, let alone at my mother's house for Sunday dinner. I had no choice but to go though. I was hungry as hell and cooking isn't something I do so if I didn't go I'd starve to death. My face had mostly gone down but my eyes were still swollen. It had taken cold compresses, rubbing alcohol and Benadryl to get my face back somewhat normal.

I hadn't been able to leave my apartment all week which put me even further behind in opening up my business. Being cooped up at home did give me time to plot my revenge against Isabel. That long neck bitch had to pay. She wanted to play dirty so I was going to play even dirtier. She had to know that I wasn't the one to play with. I wasn't scared of Isabel anymore.

Her ass was gon' learn that Sunday Rose Vasi doesn't take shit from anybody. I did however wonder how much of me and Emma's conversation she'd overheard. She had to have heard the part about me having an affair with Damon but did she hear for how long? I don't know. I couldn't concentrate on that. I would deal with Isabel later. Right now it was time to get my grub on. I hung up coat my in my mother's coat closet and made my way to the dining room.

I looked like a bum but I didn't care. My mother would of course have something to say but I didn't give a shit. She would have to deal with my ratty Run DMC tee shirt, grey joggers and Nike high top dunk sneakers. I would of course be the odd one out because Sunday dinner at the Vasi house was a formal affair. For once I wasn't late. The first course hadn't even come out of the kitchen yet.

"Hey," I waved, unenthusiastically to everyone.

My black bug-eyed Chanel shades covered my puffy swollen eyes.

"Hey sis," Tee-Tee greeted me with a warm hug. "How yo' eye feeling, girl?"

"The same way yo' face is gonna feel if you don't leave me the hell alone." I playfully pushed him away.

"Hey Mase," I kissed Dylan's cute 2 year old son on the cheek. "Is he feeling better?" I asked, Dylan.

"Yeah, much better. How are you?" She asked, concerned.

"I feel like shit."

"Watch your mouth little girl." My mother sauntered into the dining room with a glass of Jack Daniels in hand.

As usual my mother was tipsy but her hair was completely throwing me off. My mother resembled a Texas pageant mom. The wig she wore had a big hump at the top and a swoop bang. Whoever did her hair had to have used a whole entire bottle of Aqua Net on it. The shit looked hard as hell. She looked a hot mess.

"My bad mama." I walked over and gave her a light hug.

"Thank god, I have my drink in my system 'cause your attire this evening is giving me the blues." She pursed her lips.

"Good to see you too, mama." I patted her on the back. "Where is my niece?"

"Upstairs sleep," Bernard replied.

"How you doing, Sunday?" Angel hit me with a head nod.

"Hey cousin," I smiled, sitting down at the table.

"What's up wit' the shades?" He asked.

"You don't wanna know." I placed my napkin in my lap.

"Word around town is that Isabel McKnight put cucumber extract in her facial when she was at the spa." My mother laughed.

"I'm glad you find it so funny mother. That Shirley Caesar wig you got on your head is even funnier," I countered.

"Excuse you… my hair looks good." She tried to run her fingers through the crispy wig but found it difficult.

"Whoever did that to your hair needs to be shot," I snickered.

"Grow up, Sunday." My mother rolled her eyes.

"You first." I shot back.

"Hello family!" My daddy declared with his much younger girlfriend ZaShontay on his arm.

I honestly don't know if my daddy is going through a mid life crisis or not. I never imagined him dating someone younger, let alone as ghetto as ZaShontay. The chick looked like a walking Charlotte Russe ad. She was pretty as hell. She reminded me of Meagan Good but her over-the-top style distracted you from her beauty. ZaShontay had 32 inch purple weave in her head and purple lipstick with black lip liner on her lips.

She wore a floral print crop top with a pair of matching leggings, a Louis Vuitton belt and 6 inch spiked Louboutin platform heels. Her stiletto nails had to be at least 35 inches long and her big Tahiry size ass bounced whenever she walked. It had to be her ass that had my dad hypnotized because ZaShontay wasn't offering much in the mental department. The funny thing about my dad bringing her to dinner was that my mother was sure to have a heart attack. I was happy as hell to have a front row seat for the showdown.

"Hey ya'll," ZaShontay waved, smacking her gum.

"Eric, have you lost your damn mind?" My mother stood from her seat. "How dare you bring this hussy into my home?"

"Who you calling a hussy?" ZaShontay swung her weave to the side. "Ain't no horse in my head. This here is Brazilian weave, ma'am."

"Jesus be a fence." Dylan held her head down and laughed.

"Whaaaat?" ZaShontay screwed up her face, trying to figure out what was funny.

"Can you please date someone with a higher education than the 5th grade?" My mother scoffed, sitting back down.

"Uh excuse you. I got my GED. You betta tell her Eric. I don't play." ZaShontay pulled out a pink stun gun. "I will sting her ass."

"Not if I shoot you first." My mother pulled her pocket pistol from underneath the table.

"Lane, put that gun up. It's not even loaded." My father demanded, escorting ZaShontay to her seat.

"How you been daddy?" I asked.

"Great, baby girl. ZaShontay makes sure that I'm eating right and taking my medication. Having her in my life has been such a blessing." My dad glared at my mother.

"Chile please," Lane waved him off.

"I can't have big daddy long stroke kickin' it wit' Jesus just yet." ZaShontay kissed my father on the lips.

Everyone at the table cringed. I think I'ma throw up. Did this chick just call my 56 years old father big daddy long stroke? Eww.

"Rosa!" Lane yelled over her shoulder. "Bring out all three courses at once! I want this dinner over with as soon as possible! And Sunday you know better. Take your glasses off while you're in the house."

"I can't mama." I replied, taking a sip of my drink.

"Oh but you will. I taught you better manners than that."

"My glasses stay on," I spoke, unyielding.

"Leave the girl alone, Lane." My dad said.

"You hush." My mother pointed her knife in his direction.

"Ugh, why she so violent? Must be that time of the month or menopause." ZaShontay picked at her nails.

"You have until the count of three to take those goddamn glasses off." My mother leaned over into my face. "One... two..."

"Ok!" I yelled taking off my shades.

"Oh hell naw! Put them glasses back on!" Angel winced along with everyone else.

My whole entire family got to witness my fucked up face. My eyes looked like two red marshmallows. My eyelids and underneath my eyes were swollen.

"You happy now?" I barked at my mama.

"Gosh no. Put them back on." My mother turned her head in disgust.

"You should've listened to me the first time." I placed my shades back over my eyes.

"Isabel sure did a number on you." My mother tuned up her face.

"Oh we got something for that heffa." Tee-Tee wagged his tongue and raised his hand for a five.

"You damn right we do." I gave him a high-five.

"What we gon' do?" He whispered.

"I don't know. I thought you had a plan," I giggled.

"You ready for your next date, Sunday? My boy Cliff can't wait to meet you," Bernard said.

"I use to fuck wit' a nigga name Cliff." ZaShontay chimed in. "He stay on the Westside?"

127

"Nah," Bernard shook his head appalled.

"What kind of old ass name is Cliff?" Dylan laughed.

"Leave my boy name alone. Cliff is a cool dude, man. He's going to show Sunday a good time," Bernard assured. "So Sunday you ready?"

"I guess I'm ready." I tried to convince myself.

The only reason I was still going through with these stupid dates is because I needed something to distract me from pining after Damon. I wasn't going to allow myself to get caught up in him again. Loving him was a death trap. Maybe Cliff would be the answer to all of my problems. Maybe just maybe he would be the man of my dreams.

Quit fuckin' wit' them lames, right now. I can put you up on game, right now.

-PartyNextDoor, "Right Now"

Chapter 9

So it's Valentine's Day and I find myself sitting alone at Mango restaurant gazing out of the window. My date Cliff was twenty minutes late and hadn't even called to explain why. He had five more minutes to arrive and I was going to order my food. A chick like me ain't got time to be waiting. My fat ass is hungry. Mango had the best authentic Peruvian food in town. Nestled downtown in the Washington Avenue loft distract; where I stayed, Mango featured an upscale, loft style environment. The restaurant had a cozy sultry vibe to it.

I was on my second glass of Pinot Nior and was becoming quite tipsy due to the fact I hadn't eaten all day. I was trying to make sure that my stomach was extra flat that night. I wore a see through short sleeve shirt with a black racerback bralette underneath. A pair of tight leather Rick Owens leggings hugged my thighs and legs. On my feet were a pair of 4 ¾ inch Giuseppe Zanotti suede ankle strap booties. I accessorized my look with a pair of gold Jennifer Fisher batwing earrings with pave white diamonds and a matching necklace. On my wrist was a vintage gold Rolex watch.

When I walked into the restaurant everybody stared at me like I was a movie star. All of the attention I was receiving made me feel special. Starving myself all day had paid off. For a brief moment I was on a natural high. Then Cliff didn't show up on time and I became irate. I mean the man's name was already Cliff. He didn't need another strike against him. I hated when folks were late. The shit was incredibly rude and annoying as hell. I was simply too cute to be sitting alone on Valentine's Day in a nice restaurant waiting on a nigga named Cliff.

People were starting to whisper and stare. I felt like a complete loser. I was embarrassed as hell. What was even worse was that I hadn't heard from Damon all day. He'd been blowing me up since the reunion but today, I hadn't heard from him once. We'd talked several times prior to today via Facetime. He'd shown me his new bachelor pad but I refused to see him. Maybe my resistance pushed him away but still it was Valentine's Day. If he loved me as much as he said he did then he should've reached out to me.

Deciding I'd be nosey, I pulled out my phone and logged on to Instagram. Damon didn't have an IG page but Isabel did. *IsabelTheGreat* was her IG name. She had over 100,000 followers. The heffa had more followers than me. Bitch. As soon as I clicked on her page I didn't have to search far. The last picture she posted was a pic of Damon and their two girls. Damon was smiling brightly while holding his girls in his arms. The girls held pink balloons and heart shaped boxes of chocolate in their hands. The caption underneath the pic read:

The loves of my life.

The second to last picture was of Isabel's engagement ring. Apparently it had been upgraded and the caption underneath the picture read:

My husband always knows how to make me happy.
Best Valentine's Day ever!!! :)

My heart was crushed. Damon hadn't called me because he was with his family. His family came first and apparently Isabel was still his family. I was so stupid to have even remotely entertained him and his lies. Nothing about Damon had changed. He was still on the same bullshit. Thank god, I was meeting up with Cliff. I deserved to be loved whole heartedly by a man. I was nobody's second choice. Hurt, I threw my phone back inside my purse and looked out the window.

I became mortified when I saw a pimped out old school, neon yellow, Cadillac sitting on dubs pull into the parking lot. I couldn't believe my eyes. Lord please, don't let this be my date. I do not have time for the bullshit. The owner of the car stepped out looking like an extra from the HBO documentary *Pimps Up, Hoes Down*.

The man looked to be in his forties. He was 5'3 with dark skin and a baby fro. That wasn't the bad part. The outfit he was wearing was what fucked me up. This negro had on a sky blue Steve Harvey suit. He wore a powder blue button up, matching tie, sky blue vest, a matching suit jacket that reached right above his ankles, a pair of wide leg slacks and a pair of white Stacy Adam shoes.

No-no-no this can't be happening. This country negro bet not be Cliff. Lord please, don't do this to me. My prayers unfortunately weren't answered. Before I could make a quick escape the man dressed like a Smurf was in my face. There was no where for me to escape. The entrance door was too far away. I couldn't pretend like he had the wrong person either. We were the only black people in the entire restaurant.

"Ooooooh wee." Cliff snapped his finger. "Girl, you lookin' good enough to eat. Stand up and let Cliff look at ya'." He pulled me out of the booth without my permission.

Cliff spun me around and examined my frame.

"Damn that ass sitting!" He popped me on the butt with his hand.

I was so flabbergasted that I couldn't even react the way I wanted to, which was a swift kick to the face.

"Please don't touch me again." I shot him a look that could kill.

"My bad." Cliff placed his hands up in the freeze position. "No disrespect, shawty. When Cliff like what he see, Cliff can't help his self." He sucked his teeth and took his seat.

I sat back down and literally had to will myself not to cry. My life ain't shit. Who else on the planet has this much bad luck? No one! I bet the Cashmere Mafia has put a hex on me. That has to be it.

"You ordered yet?" Cliff looked over the menu.

"No. I was waiting on you," I stressed with an attitude.

"Aww shit girl. You should'a been ate. A nigga like Cliff always late. Cliff gotta make sure his fit is right before Cliff dot that door." He popped his collar.

"This is some bullshit," I mumbled, underneath my breath.

"What you say love muffin?"

"Nothing." I faked a smile.

"What in the shit is on this menu? Cliff ain't never heard of no damn Ceviche de Pescado. Cliff don't fuck wit' no foreign food. What we should've ate was Sweetie Pies. That right there is the truth."

"Sweetie Pies is good." I agreed not knowing what else to say.

135

"Can I get you something to drink, sir?" The waiter asked.

"Ya'll got any Yak back there?"

I can't. I simply can't.

"Excuse me?" The waiter asked confused.

"He'll have a Hennessey and coke and for our entrée we'll have the Sattado de Langostinos," I said to the waiter.

"Coming right up." The waiter took our menus away.

"Ok." Cliff leaned back. "Cliff see you. Cliff like a woman that takes the initiative."

"Oh my god," I asked, unable to help myself. "Please explain to me why you keep referring to yourself in the third person?"

"Cliff doesn't know what you're talking about." He looked at me with a puzzled expression on his face.

For a brief second, I sat with my mouth open.

"Never mind," I waved him off feeling like my head was about to explode.

"So tell me sugafoot. Why is a dimepiece like you single?"

"Cause all of the men I meet smell like falafels and fungus." I replied, sarcastically.

It drove me insane when a man asked me why I was single. Men these days act like being single is the plague. Like, you're one step away from death. I'm single obviously because I haven't found the right person, duh!

"Why are you single?" I couldn't resist asking.

"Oh, I'm not single. My main bitch back at the crib," Cliff replied, not missing a beat.

I know, I didn't just hear him right.

"You say what now?" I placed my finger up to my ear and leaned forward to hear him better.

"Aww yeah, Cliff loves the ladies and the ladies love Cliff. Gone head and hop on the train. Choo-choo!" He blew a make believe horn as our food arrived.

"No thank you. I'd rather jump to my death." I placed my napkin on my lap.

"Yous a feisty one, huh? Cliff like that." He gave me a devilish grin and proceeded to eat his food.

Cliff ate his food with his fingers and every five seconds he'd lick his fingers instead of wiping them on his napkin. My food looked delicious but he was making my stomach turn with his poor eating habits.

"Are your parents related?" I died to know.

"Hell to the naw! Why you say that?" Cliff asked with sauce all over his lips.

"You just seem like the perfect example of what happens when first cousins marry," I declared, feeling sick to my stomach.

Cliff looked at me confused. Once again my sarcasm had flown over his head.

"So uh after dinner you gon' let old Cliff here click yo' mouse?" He winked his eye at me.

"What?" I asked draining my glass of wine.

"Can Cliff refresh yo' page?" He sucked his teeth.

"What?"

"Can Cliff download yo' document?" He whispered in a sexy tone.

"I don't understand what you're saying, sweetie. Speak English please," I demanded.

"You gon' let Cliff get in them draws or nah?" He said so loud everyone in the restaurant turned and looked at us.

"Check please!" I raised my hand, signaling the waiter.

I'd had enough!

"Awwwww shit! It's about to go down. Let Cliff finish his food first." He danced in his seat.

"Ain't shit going down. I'm getting the fuck away from you! This date is over, sir."

I couldn't take it anymore. I refused to spend another minute of my life with this clown.

"What's wrong? Cliff thought we were connecting." He said, sincerely.

"I don't know where you got that shit from." I corrected him.

"Here you go sir." The waiter placed the check down in front of Cliff.

"Let Cliff get a to-go-box, please." He said to the waiter while picking up the bill. "Oooooh that's steep." He passed the bill across the table to me.

"What am I supposed to do with this?" I held the check up in my hand.

"You gon' pay the bill. Cliff got to be at least ten dates in before he start trickin'. You done lost yo' mind. You fine and all but don't get it twisted." He picked his teeth with his fork.

"Somebody call 911 'cause I'm about to kill him," I exclaimed, heated.

The bill was only $69.58. This nigga couldn't pay sixty-nine damn dollars. I didn't hate anyone but this nigga had me all the way fucked up. One thing is for certain. I'm going to kill Bernard. As soon as I leave this freakin' restaurant I'm going to drive over to my brother's house and slap the holy shit outta Bernard. What was he thinking setting me up with this bad-body, lousy ass nigga?

Pissed to the highest extent, I pulled out my black American Express card. As I went to hand the waiter the bill back it was taken out of my hand by no other than Blue. Really Jesus? Blue had literally appeared like a ghost. A sexy ghost none the less. He donned an army green button up that was buttoned all the way up to the collar. A thin gold rope chain rested on his chest. A nice pair of dark denim jeans and a pair of red, white and black high top Nike Dunks completed his simplistic look.

"I got this." He handed the waiter $200. "Keep the change."

"Thank you sir." The waiter said, giddily.

"Happy Valentine's Day, miss lady." Blue handed me a bouquet of pink tulips.

"How did you know I was here?" I smiled, taking the flowers.

141

"A little birdie told me." He referred to Dylan. "Scoot over."

Blue eased his way into the booth.

"Is this the rapper Blue?" Cliff asked astonished.

"Yeah, it's me," Blue responded.

"Awwww shit. Cliff fuck hoes to your music all the time. What it do man?" Cliff dapped Blue up.

"What up?" Blue grinned.

"Now hold up Kit Kat." Cliff froze in a panic. "Cliff ain't into no threesomes at least not wit' no dude. Cliff done dabbled a little bit back in the day but that was during my experimental faze. Cliff likes to tap that ass. He don't like to get his booty tapped no more."

"Who is this guy and why are you with him?" Blue asked, puzzled.

"It's a long story." I shook my head embarrassed.

"Aye bruh, I got it from here. You can head on out." Blue commanded.

"Well…" Cliff picked up his to-go-box. "I've been kicked out of far better threesomes. I don't even know why you're even wasting your time on her. She ain't giving up no ass. Cliff bids you ado." Cliff curtsied on his way out the door.

"Thank god, he's gone," I exhaled, relieved. "I feel like I just went through child birth."

"You gon' get enough fuckin' wit' these lames."

"You don't know who I mess with, stalker," I nudged his arm with my shoulder.

"I know enough after seeing you with that nigga. You too damn cute to be paying the bill for some dude in a pimp suit." Blue's hazel eyes sparkled.

"Tell me about it. Thank you for the flowers and dinner," I laughed, nervously. "So it took you over a month to find me, huh?"

"Nah, I've just been real busy on my promotional tour for my new album. I've had my eye on you though."

"Ok creep," I joked.

"You know you happy to see me."

143

I wasn't going to admit it to Blue but ironically enough I was super pleased to be in his company. The man looked and smelled delicious. His massive physical presence was making my lady parts moist. I wondered did he know that if he tried he could get it how he wanted it?

"It's cool," Blue licked his bottom lip. "You ain't gotta admit it. I can see it in your eyes. You miss me."

"Whatever." I tried my damnest not to hop on his lap and ride his dick. "How long are you in town?"

"Just for the night. I came into town specifically to see you." He confessed.

Did my heart just drop down to my clit 'cause it sure feels like it did?

"Wow," I responded speechless. "That's really sweet."

"C'mon," Blue took me by the hand. "Let's get out of here. I wanna take you some place."

I just love when I'm wit' you.
Yeah, this shit is on 10.

-Drake, "Wu-Tang Forever"

Chapter 10

If I could describe my night with Blue in one word it would be magical. Before I even had time to think I was being whisked away in his Mercedes Benz G Wagon. I didn't know where we were going. Blue refused to tell me. I prayed to god that his ass wasn't crazy. For all I knew, he could've been some psycho killer. Blue was cool, though. He was the perfect gentleman. I sat comfortably in the passenger seat. The warm heat coming from the vents blew against my skin.

He and I speed along the highway bumpin' Andre 3000's *She Lives In My Lap*. The sexy erotic song mixed with Blue's captivating presence had me feeling some type of way. Blue was everything I was trying to avoid. Nothing good could come from a nigga like him. He was charming and sweet now but sooner or later his inner asshole would take over again. This knight in shining armor act he was putting on was just a front. But as he gripped the steering wheel with his strong hands and looked over at me, all I could imagine was him gripping my thighs while I sucked on his bottom lip.

Get it together, Sunday. Yeah, he's big as hell with muscular legs and had a beard you want to run your fingers though but he's a rapper. He ain't to be trusted. Just enjoy his company and keep it moving. After a fifteen minute drive we arrived at Lambert airport. Blue pulled his car into a secluded parking lot.

"You trying to get us locked up?" I looked around for the police.

"Trust me, we're good." Blue put the car into park and turned the ignition off.

He left the radio on. D'Angelo's *Lady* had begun to play.

"What are we doing here? We about to go on a trip?" I asked perplexed.

"Lay your seat back."

"Oh hell naw," I spazzed out. "If you think we're about to smash, you got another thing coming."

"If I wanted to have sex with you, I would'a been had sex with you. Just lay your seat all the way back," Blue ordered.

I don't know why but when Blue spoke my hard headed ass listened. I did as I was told and lay my seat back. Blue opened the sunroof then he lay back.

"Ok what are we looking at?" I remarked, clasping my hands together. "'Cause I'm not big on the whole sun, moon, stars, galaxy thing. Mother earth really doesn't move me."

"Just shut up and look," Blue chuckled.

I gazed up at the sky unimpressed. A minute went by where I lie there impatiently waiting for something mesmerizing to happen when it did. Out of nowhere a plane that was taking off flew right over us. I mean it was so close, I felt I could reach out and touch it. The sheer vibration of the plane alone was enough to send me on an orgasmic high. It was one of the dopest things I'd ever witnessed in my life.

"Oooooh make it do it again." I clapped my hands like a little kid.

"That shit was hot, right?" Blue shined his infamous crooked grin.

"Yeah, how do you even know about this spot?"

"I've been coming here since I was a kid." Blue became serious. "My father is a pilot. He used to bring me and my brother here all the time to watch the planes take off."

"Wow, that's so cool. I can't get over it. That was so dope," I smiled, reeling from the experience.

"I figured you'd like it." He said after a pause.

"I loved it," I said sincerely, gazing into his hazel eyes.

Blue looked back into mine. An undeniable attraction was brewing between him and me. No matter how much I fought it, I liked him. Blue was kinda winning my heart. The sound of my phone notifying me that I had a text message broke our gaze.

"Let me get that." I sat up and reached for my purse.

I'd received a message from Damon.

Today 10:26 PM

Happy Valentine's Day, baby. I love u

Bye Fe'Damon! This nigga must think I'm the dumbest bitch on the planet. Valentine's Day was damn near over and this nigga was just not reaching out to me. Boy bye! Ain't nobody got time for that bullshit. What made it even more fucked up was that he texted me instead of picking up the phone to call. The text only led me to believe that he was still with Isabel, instead of being at home where he should've been. Heated, I angrily responded back.

Today 10:27PM

FUCK OFF!!!!!!

I knew my response was going to infuriate Damon so I blocked his calls for the rest of the night. That'll teach his ass to fuck with me.

"You good?" Blue asked.

"Yea, I'm fine," I lied, placing my phone back in my purse.

Fixing my attitude, I lay back in my seat and looked up at the stars. It was a clear winter's night. The stars twinkled like diamonds.

"So what's up wit' you having one year to find a husband or you're going to go through with fertility treatments?" Blue asked, intrigued.

"Oh my lord, I swear my family talks too much," I groaned, embarrassed.

"The only reason I ask is because you're so young. You're only thirty, right?"

"Yeah," I nodded. "It's just that I really want a family. I really wanna be a mom and once a woman gets into her thirties each year her chances of conceiving decreases. Plus my track record with men hasn't been so good. I'm just tired of waiting on Mr. Right to magically appear. I figured, I'd take matters into my own hands and see what happens."

"How is that working out for you?" Blue asked with a laugh.

"Uhhhhhh," I laughed. "As you can see by tonight… not so good."

"Damn so I ain't even in the running?" Blue said taken aback by my response.

"No-no-no-no," I laughed uncontrollably. "It's not even like that. I'ma keep it all the way 100 wit' you. When we first met of course I was attracted to you. I mean who wouldn't be. Look at you."

"Ya' boy is kind of fine," Blue nodded in agreement.

"Whatever anyway," I ignored his sarcasm. "To me you came across very arrogant and conceited. Besides that I've dated your kind before when I lived out in L.A."

"What exactly is my kind?" Blue's voice was low and raspy.

"The industry dude that's always in the club, poppin' bottles, fuckin' one chick after another. Women are disposable to men like you. I'm trying to be someone's everything not their just for the moment." I confessed whole heartily.

"I'm happy to hear you know me so well," Blue said sarcastically. "I hate to hurt your feelings lil' mama but you got me all wrong. I apologize for the way I came at you that night. But askin' you can I have a dance ain't all that original. I ain't wanna come across lookin' like no lame so I got your attention the best way I know how."

"By being an asshole," I giggled.

"Hey, being an asshole has opened a lot of doors for me. I mean look… it got you here with me right now." He pointed out.

"You're right." I had to agree.

"But don't let what I do for a living sway your opinion of me. I can't lie when I first got in the game; I was fuckin' hoes left and right. That shit got old quick. I'm

153

older now and I get tired of coming home to an empty crib."

"You wanna have kids?" I asked, loving the sight of his face.

"At least five of 'em."

"Five?! You have lost your mind?"

"What's wrong with five kids?" Blue cocked his head back.

"Nothing, but you ain't gon' have my sweet vag all loose and deformed from pushing out five big head babies," I joked.

"Oh so you gon' be the mother of my kids?" Blue caught me.

Fuck!

"Who knows what the future may hold," I grinned, trying to play it off.

"Uh huh, that's what's up," Blue grinned. "But nah for real, I'm feeling you. Ain't no games or gimmicks here.

I'm just a handsome ass guy trying to get to know a very pretty girl."

My simple ass loved it when a man told me I was pretty.

"I hear you but you still out here wildin' out on dudes in the streets. Didn't I just see you on World Star Hip Hop, video taping yourself beating up some dude out in the Hollywood Hills?"

"Oh yeah, that had to go down. The nigga was getting way out of line so I had to set him straight," Blue declared with no remorse.

"See that's the stuff I'm talking about. You rappers are crazy. We are damn near fifty. Who has time to be fighting?" I challenged.

"You're right but I'm a man and certain things just can't be ignored. Look it happened." He reasoned, giving me full eye contact.

"I can't take it back nor do I want to. If some clown ass nigga is coming at me or my family sideways I'ma handle it, flat out. But understand that if you were my lady,

I would never put you in harms way. You're far too precious for that."

Ok Blue. Keep on saying all the right things. The real test would be would his actions match his words?

"When is the next time you'll be back in town?" I questioned.

"Shit… it'll be at least a month or so. My schedule is jam packed. What? You wanna see me again?" Blue shot me a mock-glare and smiled.

"Maybe." My face turned bright red.

"I got yo' ass missing a nigga already," he chuckled.

"Stop. You ain't got me like that," I disagreed.

"Oh, I don't?" Blue leaned over and planted a deep sensual kiss on my lips.

I'd never been kissed with so much intensity in my life. It was like he'd been craving me for decades and was finally getting a taste. Blue held my face in his hands and I drowned in his touch. There underneath the stars Blue's tongue danced slowly with mine. What we were creating was the shit I read about in books or saw on the big screen. Stuff like this didn't happen to women like me.

As we kissed another plane flew over us. Blue pulled me close. My chest was pressed up against his. I never wanted to leave his arms. He'd done it. Somehow with one kiss, with one flicker of his tongue Blue had done the impossible. He'd made me fall for him.

Fuck what you heard, you're mine.

-Beyoncé feat Drake, "Mine"

Chapter 11

Unfortunately, my blissful night with Blue had to come to an end. I didn't it want to. We had so much fun together. All night, I made him laugh and he made me smile and blush. For hours we lie underneath the stars talking about our goals, fears, desires, our childhood and more. After a while I became famished.

Blue took me to a nice, quaint place called Benton Park Café. The cafe was open 24 hours and served breakfast all day which was a plus for me. I loved breakfast. I ordered the Ultimate Benedict which was a dope play on the classic Eggs Benedict. Benton Park's version was a toasted English muffin, two poached eggs, hollandaise sauce, sautéed spinach, tomato, bacon and avocado. FYI the shit was fuckin' delicious! Blue didn't even mind when I found myself still hungry and wanted more to eat.

He actually liked that I was a woman who liked to eat. He and I happily split a gigantic pancake and a bowl of fresh fruit. It was nearly 6:00a.m by the time I got home. When Blue dropped me back off to my car, it was time for him to catch his flight. Blue seductively pressed me up against the driver side door of my car and wrapped his arms around my waist.

I locked my fingers around in his neck and stood on my tippy toes to kiss him goodbye. As our lips touched, I found myself not wanting him to leave. If he would've asked me to accompany him on his tour, I would've but we both had shit to do. We sealed our goodbye with a kiss and promised to stay in touch until next time. Our next rendezvous couldn't come fast enough.

Blue had changed my entire perception of him. He was a gentle giant with a hard exterior. With him I felt important. He made me feel like my thoughts mattered to him. Being with him was effortless. I wouldn't trade the memories I made with Blue that night for all of the Chanel in the world. For the first time in a long time I felt like a princess and it was all because of him.

It was a little after 9:00a.m and I was knocked out sleep in bed. The sleep I was in felt better than sex. After being out all night, I needed the rest. I hadn't even bothered putting on pajamas. As soon as I got home I stripped down to my black lace panties and bra set and went straight to bed. I had no plans on getting up until mid-afternoon but my plans were derailed when I heard someone banging on my door.

Agitated, I snatched the covers from over my head and looked at the clock. When I realized that I'd only been asleep for a few hours and was being awakened by some deranged person, I flipped. Fuming, I pulled the covers from over my body and stomped to the door. Whoever was on the other side of the door was about to get royally cussed the fuck out. On my tip toes I peeked out the peep hole and found Damon.

"Fuck," I whispered, placing my back up against the door.

I wasn't in the mood for Damon today. I jut wanted to sleep. That's it.

"Open the door, Sunday! I know you're standing there!" He barked.

161

Here he go.

"Can you come back later? I'm trying to sleep." I finally answered.

"Open the fuckin' door!" He banged his fist against the door causing it to rattle.

Oh so this nigga wanna shake the door.

"I'm not playin' wit' you Sunday! I will wake everybody in this muthafuckin' up!" Damon threatened.

Knowing he wasn't joking, I unwilling unlocked the door. I didn't even bother opening it for him. I walked my ass back to my room and left him to fend for his self. Damon opened the door and locked it behind him.

"You really need to grow up." He shot following me.

"Ain't that the pot calling the kettle black," I scoffed, switching extra hard.

"So you gon' tell me to fuck off last night then block me from calling you?" He demanded to know.

"Damn, I forgot all about that," I laughed, getting back into bed.

"Oh so you think that shit is funny? I've been calling you all fuckin' night!" Damon pulled the covers back forcefully.

"Somebody's mad." I mocked him.

Damon stood quiet. He was heated but the sight of my half naked physique did something to him. I could see something click in his brain. I had to admit my body was looking right. My tits were sitting pretty in my bra and my full thighs were begging him to stick his face in-between them.

"I'm tired of playing of these games wit' you, Sunday." He took off his cashmere trench coat and threw it across the room.

"You're the one playing games Damon not me." I yawned not here for his dramatic behavior.

"I text you and tell you Happy Valentine's Day and that I love you and you tell me to fuck off? What kind of shit is that?" He loosened his tie and removed it.

"You damn right, I told you to fuck off." I responded ready to flip.

Not in the mood for Damon and his shenanigans, I tried to pull the covers back up but he wouldn't allow me. Damon was so mad he took my comforter and sheet off the bed and flung it across the room. This nigga is crazy.

"That was stupid," I shot.

"Don't tell me fuck off again. I'm not playin' wit' you!" Damon barked.

"You didn't hit me up until damn near midnight to tell me Happy Valentine's Day." I sat up straight. "Then you text me on top of that instead of calling me? You would've been better off not reaching out to me all."

"I had every intention on reaching out to you but I got caught up." Damon took off his shirt and let it drop to the floor.

"Yeah, you got caught alright. You got caught up wit' yo' bitch. By the way I love the new upgrade on her ring. That shit was hot." I shot sarcastically. "When you slept over last night did you fuck her?"

"What makes you think I spent the night?" Damon folded his arms across his broad chest.

"C'mon Damon, I'm far from stupid." I lie back down. "You hit me up via text last night 'cause you were still with her."

"Actually, I was wit' my kids. The girls are having a hard time adjusting to the separation and begged me to stay so I did. I slept in the guest room, though."

"I don't give a damn where you slept. You weren't in the bed with me so fuck what you're talkin' about!" I retorted, resentfully."

Instead of responding Damon unbuttoned his pants and slid them off.

I hated that my eyes went directly to the thick bulge in his boxer/briefs. The imprint of Damon's dick looked like two big fist.

"What are you doing?" I looked at him confused.

"I'm about to fuck the shit outta you but before I do lets get a couple of things straight." Damon pulled his underwear off.

His long dick slapped against his thigh. My mouth watered. This nigga wasn't playing fair. He knew I couldn't resist a big dick. Damon caught me staring at his dick and grinned. Stroking his dick he lay on top of me.

"I didn't upgrade Isabel's ring. She did with my money." He spoke between kissing my lips.

"That's why she put that stupid ass post up. She was trying to get back at me for moving out. Now look, I'm tried of telling you that all I want is you." Damon looked me square in the eyes.

His gaze was so intense I became choked up. Why does this man have this effect on me?

"Isabel and I are over. She knows this. She knows that I love you. That's why she pulled that shit wit' you at the spa." Damon slid my panties to the side.

"Ah uh," I shook my head. "I am not about to fuck you."

"You ain't?" Damon slid his dick up and down my wet slit.

Juices immediately started to flow from my walls.

I love you, Sunday Rose Vasi. You," he plunged his dick deep inside my pussy.

I gasped for air and held on tight. Lord, help me.

"When are you gon' realize that?" Damon gripped both of my thighs.

"Fuck," I whispered, feeling myself fall down the rabbit hole again.

Damon rested his forehead against mine and grinded his hips in a circular motion. This was not how I envisioned my morning. I was supposed to be sleep, not moaning in sheer agony from the width and length of Damon's dick. I'd sworn him off. Yet, here I was clawing his back and begging for mercy.

"I'm tried of going back and forth with you." He sped up his pace.

"You gon' learn to stop playing with me." Damon flipped me over onto my stomach.

The room was spinning. I could've sworn I saw Venus, Jupiter and Mars. Damon held the cheeks of my ass in his hands and rammed his dick in and out of my wet hole at a feverish pace. My entire bed was rocking. I couldn't take it. His dick felt like a combination of heaven and hell.

"Ahhhhhhhhh fuck me!" I buried my face inside my pillow.

Damon unsnapped my bra and I gladly threw it on the floor.

"Shit, Damon! Ahhhhhhhhhhhhhhhhhhhhhhhh! Fuck me boy! Fuck me daddy!" I threw my ass into his shaft.

"You gon' be a good girl from now on?" He slapped my right ass cheek.

"Yes," I groaned, feeling myself about to cum.

"You ain't gon' act up no more?" He slapped my other ass cheek even harder.

"No!" I closed my eyes tight and called out for god.

"Good." He thrust his dick one last time and came inside of me.

Cumming too, I let out a loud wail as my body convulsed. This shit wasn't fair. Who told this nigga to come over here and fuck me like that? I know I didn't but goddamn was it good. Damon knew how to torture, tease and please me all at the same time. Spent we both lie paralyzed, catching our breath. Damon lay on his back.

His dick stood in the air. It was still hard. If I wasn't so tired, I would've leaned over and took him in my mouth. But now wasn't the time for oral pleasure. This nigga was still on punishment. Just 'cause he'd fucked me to outer space and back didn't mean nothing.

"Where were you last night?" Damon turned to me and asked.

"At home, why?" I lied, panting.

"Lie again!" Damon pinched my nipple.

"Owwww nigga that hurt," I screeched, slapping him hard on the arm. "I'm not lying to you."

"Sunday, I see your clothes from last night on the floor." He pointed.

"Damn, I forgot about that," I giggled.

"Where were you?" He shot sternly.

"I went out."

"Where?"

"On a date," I smirked, loving that he was jealous.

"Didn't I tell you to cut that shit out?" Damon mean-mugged me.

"You ain't my damn, daddy," I spat.

"I was a minute ago."

"Boy bye," I laughed, waving him off.

"Who you go out with?"

"Nobody special," I replied, thinking of Blue.

For some reason, I felt like I was betraying him by sleeping with Damon. But neither of them were my man. I didn't owe either of them anything. Yet, I felt like I did.

"You gon' cut out all this date shit. Hand me my coat," Damon demanded.

You betta get yo' life." I shot him a dirty look and reached over the bed to get his coat.

"Here!" I threw it at him.

"Thank you." Damon went inside his coat pocket and pulled out a small box.

"Happy Valentine's Day." He handed the box to me.

I started at Damon quizzically before taking it. The box was a ring box.

"Is this what I think it is?" I asked, shaking.

My heart was beating a mile a minute.

"Just open it."

I reluctantly took the box from his hand and cracked it open. Inside was the most magnificent ring I'd ever seen. It was a 6.1 Harry Winston pink diamond. The ring was worth more than two million dollars. Tears flowed from my eyes. For the first time in my life I was actually speechless. This shit can't be real. This couldn't be what I thought it was but then Damon said the four words I'd been dying to hear from him my whole entire life.

"Will you marry me?"

Tears filled my throat. I couldn't speak. This was all too much. I was just mad at him. Hell, I was just with another nigga last night. He was just with his wife. We weren't even in a relationship. He was married for god sake! How could I possible say yes? I couldn't. I'd just kissed Blue. Visions of him still danced in my mind. The taste of him still lingered on my tongue. Damon was moving entirely too fast. I needed time to think.

"Well?" He asked, placing the ring on my finger.

"I don't know what to say?" I stared at the ring.

It sparkled underneath the light from the morning sun.

"Say yes." Damon pulled me into his embrace.

"I can't." My bottom lip trembled.

"Why not?"

"It's just too much too soon. I don't even know what we are yet." I responded, finding it hard to speak.

"I told you, you're mine. I'm yours right?" Damon quizzed.

I couldn't say yes. My heart was all over the place.

"Damon I don't know," I hesitated.

172

"Sunday, I love you. You and I are meant to be. I've never loved anyone the way I love you. You're mine." Damon spoke into my ear.

I swallowed the huge lump in my throat.

"I hear you but we gotta fall back and look at things for what they are. You're still married."

"I know but me and Isabel are getting a divorce. Look, it's obvious that you're hesitant and I don't blame you. Just take some time and think about it." He kissed the side of my face.

"You sure?" I asked, feeling myself begin to suffocate.

"I've never been surer about anything in my life. I'm not losing you again. If it takes the rest of my life; I'm going to make you see that."

Now that we've come this far, I need to know what's gon' be my position.

-Raheem DeVaughn, "Where I Stand"

Chapter 12

I loved spending time with Damon but after three days I was ready for his ass to go home! Cabin fever had started to set in. I had to break out. I felt like he was staying around me to ensure I wouldn't go on anymore dates. He was suffocating me. I was like dude... chill. I'm not going anywhere. Monday couldn't come fast enough. When it finally rolled around and he went to work, I headed over to Emma's house.

I slipped on a white Pretty Ratchet Thingz sweatshirt, a pair of cut-off jogging pants and combat boots. I didn't even waste time putting on a coat. I didn't care that it was 32 degrees outside with 5 inches of snow on the ground. I was dying to tell someone about the proposal. My car was barely in park before I jumped out and ran inside Emma's house. For some reason Emma's door was always unlocked. I guess it's a white folks thing.

"DAMON PROPOSED TO ME!" I shouted before I realized she had company.

Sitting right next to Emma on the floor was my brother. He and Emma were having a play date with Princess Gaga and Jada. The girls sat in-between their parent's leg rolling a ball back and forth. That annoying show Yo Gabba Gabba was on.

"Aww fuck!" I groaned, realizing I'd fucked up.

"Oh so a bitch been keeping secrets." Tee-Tee rolled his neck. "Ok, I see how you do." He handed Princess Gaga the ball.

"Hi twin." I sweetly walked over and tried to hug him.

"Get yo' ass away from me." He pushed me away. "Since when you start telling Emma stuff and not me? I'm your damn twin."

"I'm sorry. I just had to keep everything under wraps for a while," I apologized.

"I figured something was going on with you two. At the reunion, ya'll were way too comfortable together and he kept on looking at you like he wanted to bang your back out," Tee-Tee teased, popping his booty.

"Forget all of that," Emma interjected. "You're kidding me, right? He did not propose to you."

"Yes, he did." I sat on the floor Indian style. "He proposed to me Friday morning." I explained the entire story.

Tee-Tee was stunned to learn that Damon and I had a three year affair.

"Girl, I had no idea this shit was going on." Tee-Tee's mouth hung open. "I didn't know you had it in you, sis." He nudged me on the arm with his shoulder and winked.

"I'm a home wrecker." I said, distraught.

"No," Tee-Tee corrected me. "You're a bitch that's taking back what is rightfully yours. I don't know why you broke up wit' his ass in the first place. That man loves you. Everybody can see it."

"You can't be serious?" Emma eyed him like he was stupid.

"He loves her but he cheated on her and had a baby on her. Where in the dictionary does that describe love? Damon's ass is a freakin' manipulator. I don't trust him and neither should you, friend," she urged.

"Girl, bump what Nancy Grace is over here talkin' about. Let's see that ring, tho." Tee-Tee lifted my left hand. "You're not wearing the ring?"

"I told you I didn't say yes. I told him I needed time to think." I reached inside my pocket and pulled out the box.

"Good, girl. That's my friend," Emma smiled, proudly.

Tee-Tee opened the box and pretended to faint.

"Elizabeth, I'm coming! Bitch! Am I lookin' at Jesus 'cause this ring is blinding the hell outta me. How in the world did you not say yes to this?" He pulled the ring out and slipped it onto his pinky finger.

"I would've said yes, went and fixed him something to eat, dropped it like it was hot on'em and gave him some awesome jawsome!" He snapped his fingers in the air.

"Umm there are children in the room," Emma covered Jada's ears. "Sunday, I'm happy you didn't say yes."

"I'm sure you are, hater," Tee-Tee stuck his tongue out at her.

"A lot comes along with her saying yes. She's going to have to deal with the wrath of Isabel; everyone's going to be talking about her and most importantly, are you really ready to play step-mother to another woman's kids?" Emma pointed out.

I hadn't even thought of that. I loved kids and desperately wanted some of my own but I didn't know how Damon's girls would receive me. If they were anything like their mother they were gonna hate me.

"Then there's this other thing. There's this guy that I like," I confessed.

"So you just rolling in niggas," Tee-Tee cracked up laughing.

"Shut up," I laughed. "No, I'm being serious. You remember the rapper Blue that Dylan set me up with?"

179

"Aww yeah, homeboy could get it." Tee-Tee popped his lips.

"I'm really starting to like him."

"That's cute," Tee-Tee dismissed my confession. "You need a man with stability. Blue is all over the place. He can't settle down and give you the family you want."

"What do you think, Emma?" I asked, helplessly.

"How does he make you feel?"

A smile quickly graced my face.

"That says it all," Emma replied with a warm smile of her own.

"The only thing is I barely know him but when I'm with him I feel... content."

"I say follow your heart," Emma suggested.

"That's the problem. Both of them are taking up space," I frowned.

"So what you gon' do?" Tee-Tee put the ring back inside the box and handed it to me.

"I don't know," I shrugged.

I was even more confused now then I was when I got to Emma's house. I loved Damon with all of my heart. He was the man of my dreams. After years of dancing around the subject he was finally making it official. I should've been on cloud nine but I wasn't. Something in my spirit didn't feel right. My mind was telling to say no but my heart was telling me to say yes.

Don't get it twisted, this my shit.
Bow down bitches.

-Beyoncé, "Flawless"

Chapter 13

I don't know why I continue to come to these things. There I was sitting at a table with a bunch of bougie overly botoxed broads, bored out of my mind. Somehow my mother had suckered me into coming to another Pink Hats function. This event was to raise money for breast cancer awareness. The cause and running into Isabel is what got me there because other than that I was not for the Tom foolery.

Outside of the fabulous décor and scrumptious food the only upside to being at the event was that I was slaying hoes. This time I wore all pink like required. I looked fab in a pale pink blazer, pale pink button up with gold tips on the collar, pink floral print skinny jeans and silver Louboutin pumps. My hair was parted down the middle and was flat ironed bone straight.

My pink diamond engagement ring matched my look perfectly. I made sure to keep my hands underneath the table so no one could see it. I didn't want anyone knowing about my "engagement" until the perfect time. I hadn't even told Damon that my answer was yes yet. I felt that Isabel should know first.

The ladies kept going on and on about my outfit. They thought it was the cutest thing ever. All of the compliments I was receiving didn't stop me from wanting to slit my wrist. The only thing these women do is talk about their husbands, kids, plastic surgery, and each other. I frankly had better things to do with my time, like start my business. But that was a whole other subject. Thank god, I had Tee-Tee and Dylan there to keep me company.

"Look at Mrs. Claudette's wig." Dylan whispered into my ear. "It's crooked and slightly tilted to the side."

Sure enough it was. I wanted to tell her but Mrs. Claudette couldn't stand me so I decided to let Mrs. Claudette and her tired wig be. While everyone around me chit chatted, I checked my phone and realized I'd received a text message from Blue.

Today 2:45PM

184

Thinking of you…

I didn't even realize it but I'd begun to blush. Blue had that effect on me.

Today 2:47PM

Hi sir… I miss u

Today 2:50PM

I miss u too miss lady

I loved that Blue was thinking of me while out on tour. Blue made an effort to reach out to me as much as possible. When we talked time stood still. Nothing else around me mattered. I was so wrapped up in thoughts of Blue that I hadn't even noticed the Cashmere Mafia walk in. As always Isabel and her minions had to make a grand entrance. It was funny to me how they had so much control over the woman.

As soon as they stepped foot inside of the room, everyone clamored over to speak to them. I wanted to throw up. I despised how everyone treated them like they were gods. Isabel and the dumbbells bled once a month just like the rest of us. Knowing Isabel she probably didn't even have a period. She probably dropped little pellets of gold every month. Once they got done with their fan club Isabel, Mirabel and Annabelle made their way over to our table. My mother being the fake messy broad she is had waved them over.

"Mrs. Vasi, you look beautiful as always." Isabel air-kissed both of my mothers' cheeks.

"Thank you darling and so do you. Sit with us please." My mother pulled out the chair next to her.

"Are you sure? We don't want to intrude." Isabel glanced over at me.

"We'll all be on our best behavior today, won't we?" My mother shot daggers at me with her eyes.

"What you lookin' at me like that for?" I questioned, furrowing my brows.

"There will be no drama today, right?" My mother said firmly.

"Ain't nobody trippin' off her." I declared with an attitude.

"Isabel, have a seat next to me. I want to discuss with you our plans for the Pink Hat's 40th anniversary soiree." My mother resumed her seat.

"Oh yes, it's our 40th anniversary, it has to be très chic." Isabel sat next to my mother and chatted with her as if they were best friends.

I swear their asses were being extra on purpose. My mother knew how much I despised Isabel and was only conversing with her to get underneath my skin. Sadly enough, the shit was working. Lane never took the time to talk to me. She never asked how my day was or how I was doing. All she did was chastise me and put me down. I never understood why.

Tee-Tee never got the same treatment. She treated him like he was a precious gem. Nothing Tee-Tee did was wrong. She didn't even lose her shit when he came out as being transgender. The only thing she asked of him was to not remove his penis. Tee-Tee respected her wishes and kept it.

To my mother, I was a complete fuck up. I was the black sheep of the family. My hair was never right, my career was a joke and I was too fat. According to my mother clumsy I didn't live up to my full potential either. She made me feel like I was a waste of goods, like I was a disgrace to the family. Even though I acted like I didn't care, I wanted my mother's approval. I wanted her to love me.

"Isabel," I said, getting her attention. "How was your Valentine's Day?"

"Oh shit," Tee-Tee scooted his chair up to the table.

My brother knew me all too well. He knew some shit was about to go down.

"How thoughtful of you to ask, Piggy." Isabel shot me a fake smile. "It was glorious if you must know. The girls, Damon and I had a fantastic day together. Damon bought the girls balloons, candy and the cutest little Chanel charm bracelets. The girls went crazy over them. They love their daddy, dearly."

"Wow… what did he get you?" I ice grilled her.

"Nothing much," she blushed. "He just upgraded my engagement ring, that's all." Isabel held up her left hand. "I've been asking him to do it for years and he finally bit the bullet and did it."

"That is fabulous." My mother took a closer look. "What is that, 4 cararts?"

"4.5 but who's counting," Isabel let out a hearty laugh.

"After the initial shock wore off well…" Isabel looked around the table at all the women. "I had to show my appreciation like any dutiful wife." She emphasized the point by glaring at me.

Isabel was making sure that I knew she'd slept with Damon. I didn't believe her though. Damon would never sleep with her then turn around and sleep with me or would he?

"How was your Valentine's Day, Piggy?" She continued on. "I hope you didn't spend it alone. I know how hard it is out here for you single women."

"You gon' take that?" Tee-Tee instigated.

"That's funny." I hung my head and laughed.

"What's funny?" Annabelle looked at me as if I had shit on my face.

"It's funny 'cause I heard… and I know how you ladies like to gossip," I glanced around the table. "But I heard that you and Damon were on the rocks. I heard he doesn't even live with you anymore."

"I don't know what you're talking about." Isabel cleared her throat.

All of the color had left her face.

"Oh, I think you do," I challenged.

"Damon and are fine. Like any marriage and I know you other ladies can attest to this, we've gone through our rough patches but we're in this for life. Nothing can tear us apart. Nothing or no one." She made it clear to me.

"Cause you see." She placed her elbows on the table and locked her fingers together. "Damon and I are rock solid. He loves me. That's why he married *me*. Nothing comes before me and nothing comes after me."

"Ok girls, that's enough." Mrs. Claudette tried to calm the situation.

But she was too late. All eyes were on us and I was too fired up to back down now.

"Is that right?" I cocked my head to the side.

"Yes," Isabel nodded.

"You say that nothing comes before you or after you, right?" I sat up in my seat.

"Did I stutter 'cause I don't think I did," Isabel asked Mirabel.

"No, you didn't." Mirabel shot me a nasty look.

"Sunday, I told you no drama." My mother warned.

Her chest was heaving up and down.

"There is no drama over here, just facts." I checked my mother.

"The only fact is that you're miserable," Isabel spat. "You were a failure in L.A. that's why you moved back home but guess what? Nobody wants you here, especially not Damon. He didn't want you back in high school and he for damn sure doesn't want you now."

"It's about to be a fight. Somebody get my cane!" Mrs. Claudette called out.

"So that's what you think, huh?" I asked with a laugh.

"That's what I know," Isabel fumed. "He thinks you're pathetic. He pity's you."

"Once again it's funny you think that," I licked my bottom lip.

"'Cause for Damon not to want me, he sholl just proposed to me a week ago. But maybe I'm just miserable and delusional. Maybe he didn't buy me this ring." I flicked my wrist like Beyoncé in the Single Ladies video.

"Damn... shit just got real." Dylan's eyes grew wide. "Is that 6.5 carat pink diamond ring?"

My cousin knew diamonds like she knew the back of her hand. The expression on everyone's face was priceless. I wished I had a camera to capture the moment. The entire room was silent. It was so quiet you could hear a

192

pin drop. For once Isabel didn't have a snappy comeback. I'd got her ass. There was nothing she could say or do.

"Tell everyone the truth Isabel. Tell everyone how you trapped Damon into marrying you knowing damn well he never loved you. Your whole entire marriage is a joke. Damon didn't upgrade your ring, you did," I shot venomously.

"When he left your house after Valentine's Day, he came home to me." I pointed to my chest. "Your husband loves me. Me, Isabel, not you. We're finally going to be together and there's nothing you can do to stop it."

Pleased with myself I sat back in my chair and raised my right eyebrow. I'd finally slayed the dragon. Crushing Isabel made me want a cigarette and I didn't even smoke.

"Why do you this? Why do you persist to 'cause trouble? Do you get off on making everyone around you miserable?" My mother asked disgusted by my behavior.

"She's lying right?" Annabelle eyed Isabel confused.

Isabel sat silent. The tears that poured from her eyes said it all. I'd ruined the fantasy she's been feeding to the world. She couldn't lie her way out of this.

"Isabel, are you alright?" My mother hugged her tight as she cried. "I am so sorry for this. I had no idea."

All of the other ladies rushed to Isabel's side to comfort her as well. She'd tortured and teased me for years but somehow she was the victim. I couldn't win for losing. The hell with these women. They were all fake as hell. I could give two shits about what they thought about me. Damon was mine first. This bitch had whore'd herself out to him and stolen my life.

Like Tee-Tee said all I was doing was reclaiming what was rightfully mine. Damon loved me and I loved him. He was going to divorce Isabel and he and I would be married. Whoever had a problem with it could suck my dick. Fuck, Isabel and her tears.

The heffa deserved to have her shit exposed. But as I received one dirty look after another my defiance deteriorated. I quickly began to feel like shit. I wasn't built for causing other people pain. The tears coming out of Isabel's eyes were real and sadly enough I'd caused them.

194

The only time we don't fight is when we're smoking or high. - Mila J, "Smoke, Drink, Break-Up"

Chapter 14

"What the fuck were you thinking?" Damon barked when I arrived at his house later on that night.

"Hello to you too," I responded, kicking off my heels.

I was in no mood to argue and fight with him. All I wanted to do was sit down and relax.

"When you are going to stop think this shit is a game?" Damon eyed me perplexed. "What possessed you to tell her we were getting engaged?"

"Umm 'cause we are," I replied, mockingly.

"Really 'cause when were you going to tell me? The last I heard from you was you were on some unsure sure type shit."

"Well, I made up my mind today." I couldn't help up laughing.

"See you think this shit funny. I've been on the phone wit' her ass all fuckin' night. She's threatening not to let me see my kids!" Damon paced and forth angrily.

I sighed and sat on the back of the couch. I never meant for things to go so far. All I wanted was to embarrass Isabel and hurt her feelings. I didn't think Damon would be punished in the process.

"Why did you do it?" He stood in front of me.

"Is it because she embarrassed you at the spa? Is that it? 'Cause I hope to god it's not," Damon pleaded, still pacing.

I ignored his line of questioning 'cause I had a question of my own.

"Did you sleep with her that night?" I asked instead.

"Really?" He stopped dead in his tracks. "Don't try to turn this shit around on me."

"Answer the damn question! Did you sleep with her that night?!" I yelled.

"What night?" He looked at me.

"Valentine's Day. Did you sleep with her?" I crossed my arms across my chest.

"No," Damon shook his head, looking away from me.

When Damon told the truth he always looked me dead in the eye. Fuck me in the ass this nigga is lying! He's fuckin' lying. Every limb in my body became weak. This trifling nigga had sex with Isabel then came over to my house the next morning and had sex with me. He and I hadn't even used a condom. I know he didn't use one with her. She was his wife. Why would he?

"You fucked her." I said, gasping for air.

"I told you, I didn't."

"I know when you're lying. You had sex with her." I held my chest. "How could you do this to me?" I dropped to my knees and began to cry.

This nigga was doing this shit to me. Once again he'd betrayed my trust. What was it about this bitch that he couldn't shake?

"What is wrong with you? Calm down." Damon got on the floor with me and held me in his arms.

"I'm not lying to you. I told you I didn't fuck her. I wouldn't do you that you. On my kids I wouldn't do that." He palmed my face with his strong hands. "Why would you even ask me that?"

"'Cause that's what Isabel told me," I wept.

"C'mon Sunday, you know she only said that shit to get under your skin. If I was still dickin' her down, I'd still be at the crib. Look where I'm at. I got my own spot. I proposed to you. I'm divorcing her. She's grasping for straws. Don't let her fuck this up for us. I finally got you back, babe. I'm not losing you." Damon placed soft sweet kiss all over my face.

His words and comforting touch eased my fears somewhat. I needed to believe that Damon was telling me the truth and nothing but the truth. I'd exposed us. There was no turning back now. We were getting married. He was marrying me. He wouldn't be marrying if he still wanted Isabel.

Isabel was just jealous that I'd won. Little ole awkward Piggy had killed the evil ice queen and got her prince charming. I had everything I ever wanted. I had my man and kids would soon follow. Isabel was not going to ruin my happily ever after. My happily ever after was just beginning.

So it's April and Damon and I have been hanging tight despite all the criticism we'd been getting. Word had spread all over St. Louis that we were together. The whole town was talking. I'd been labeled as a conniving home wrecker. One morning I went out to my car and the word whore had been key'd into the driver side door of my car.

I knew that people weren't going to receive Damon and me being together well but never did I think vandalism would come into play. I'd worked my ass for my Mercedes Benz so I was devastated to say the least. I cried for two days over it. Damon got my car fixed and insisted that I come stay with him for a while. I was a little hesitant but I knew staying with him was the right thing to do.

After cussing me out, my mother stopped talking to me. Lane not talking to me didn't bother me so much. It was actually a relief. If I had to deal with her adding salt on an already open wound I would kill myself. She'd made it clear the day after the fundraiser that she disapproved of my relationship with Damon.

She called and left me a scathing voicemail telling me that I was nothing but a glorified side chick. She said that I was a disappointment, that I was disowned and that she was writing me out of her will. She also told me that I was bitter and pathetic. I'd always thought that she felt that way about me but to hear her actually say it killed me.

I never understood why she couldn't see things from my side. She always took everyone else's side but mine. She never supported me or my choices. Nothing I did was ever good enough for her. I was over my mother and her judgment of my life. Each day that we didn't speak was heavenly. I wasn't going to lose any sleep over it.

I had enough shit to worry about. For almost two months I'd barricaded myself in the house. The only time I left was to see my brother, Emma and Dylan. I was so depressed over everything that I hadn't even bothered with *Two Hearts*. Who was going to take love advice from a woman who'd stolen another woman's husband? My

202

business was doomed. It was over before it even started so I terminated my lease and shut down business in St. Louis for good.

On top of that Damon and I stayed into it. When we weren't drinking, we were arguing or making love. It was a nonstop cycle of abuse. When he was at working late nights at the casino on Tuesdays and Thursdays I was alone. I wasn't happy but Damon was my life vest. I needed him to survive. The whole entire world was against me. He was the only person there to comfort me in my time of need. We were going to make this shit work if it was the last thing I did. We had to prove the naysayers wrong. Me and Damon were meant to be. Damon was beyond tired of staying cooped up in the house. He insisted that we show our face to the public.

"Fuck them," he said. "They'll get over it eventually."

I was unsure but being in the house 24/7 was driving me stir crazy. Damon was right. It was time to fly the coop. Spring was in fully swing. St. Louis was always glorious in the spring. People were out shopping, going to the zoo or park.

The sun was beaming brightly. There wasn't a cloud in sight. Damon and I decided to have lunch at Sub Zero in the Central West End. We sat outside eating sushi. I tried my best hide to my identity by wearing my bug-eyed Chanel shades but everyone still knew it was me.

Everyone from the waitress to a young girl walking her dog shot me nasty looks. I was super paranoid. I couldn't even eat my food and I loved sushi like a fat kid loved cake. I hadn't smiled in months and being out on this date hadn't fixed the problem, it had only magnified it. All I wanted to do was go the fuck home and watch Chrisley Knows Best.

"Why aren't you eating?" Damon chewed his food. "You love sushi."

"I'm not hungry," I responded, dryly. "Can we leave? I'm ready to go home."

"No. I'm still eating. Look babe," Damon wiped his mouth with his napkin. "I know you're a little down but you gotta snap out of it."

"That's easier said than done," I hissed.

"You didn't lose your business behind this shit. My family is looking at me like I'm crazy. My father's not even feeling me right now. Everyone in St. Louis hates me but you want me to just get over it? Yeah, okay." I sat back with an attitude.

"I ain't eating this shit." I pushed my plate away.

"For all I know somebody might've spit in it. You're not getting it as bad as I am 'cause you're St. Louis' golden boy." I made air quotes with my hand. "Everyone loves you."

"I'm catching hell too." Damon looked around to make sure no one heard him.

"I'm just not as vocal about it as you are. My oldest daughter, Gia, won't even talk to me. Isabel won't even let the girls spend the night at my house 'cause you're there so don't tell me I ain't feeling it like you." Damon barked upset.

"I'm sick of talking about this shit." He threw his napkin down on the table.

"Oh so you mad?" I drew my head back. "Well excuse me for having fuckin' feelings."

"I'm not getting ready to argue back and forth with you. That's all we've been doing since we got engaged. I just want a day of peace."

"We'll have peace once you get a divorce. What's your excuse about that this week?"

"I'm not about to do this with you," Damon refused.

"Yes you are. I'm tired of waiting," I snapped, feeling myself about to lose it.

"How many times do I have to tell you that a divorce takes time? You of all people know should know that getting a divorce from a spiteful bitch like Isabel isn't gong to be easy."

Damon did have a point. There was no way Isabel was going to give him a divorce without putting up a fight.

"I'm just tired of being sad." I looked out into space.

"Then stop being sad. It's getting on my fuckin' nerves." Damon scooted his chair back and stood up. "I'm going to the bathroom."

I looked at Damon like he had lost his ever living mind as he walked away. This nigga is crazy. I know he didn't call his self telling me off. If he was sick of my attitude then so the fuck what. He was the one that wanted to marry my ass. I didn't propose to him. He proposed to me. What did he expect for us to do, ride off into the sunset as if we hadn't committed a sin?

Nothing about us was easy nor will it ever be. I was hurting and I needed him to be there to lift me up. My whole life was in shambles behind fucking with him and this nigga didn't have a lick of compassion. As I waited eagerly for Damon to come back so I could give him a peace of mind, my phone rang. I glanced over at my screen. It was Blue calling. My heart instantly skipped a beat and my palms began to sweat. I nervously checked to make sure the coast was clear before answering. It was.

"Hello?" I answered low enough so that no one could hear.

"Hey there miss lady."

"Hi," I smiled delighted to hear his voice.

I hadn't heard from Blue in a few days. His album was out and he'd been busy doing promotional work all over the world.

"What you doing?"

"Staring at my lunch." I picked at my sushi with my chopsticks.

"That's all bad. What you're not feeling well?"

"I guess you could say that." I twisted my lips to the side.

When I talked to Blue I felt like I was in high school again.

"Well let me make you feel better. I'm in town for a few days so let me see you tomorrow."

My calendar was clear so there was no way I was going to say no.

"Sure just let me know a place and a time."

"A'ight miss lady, I'll do that. Eat ya' food, love. Whatever is troubling you, it'll be over soon. God never gives you anything you can't handle."

"Thank you for that." I relished his words before ending the call.

By the time I hung up, Damon was returning to the table.

"What you smiling at?" He noticed me grinning from ear to ear.

I hadn't even realized that I was blushing so hard.

"Nothing." I picked up a piece of sushi and popped it into my mouth.

From eight until late, I think about you.

-Beyoncé feat Drake, "Mine"

Chapter 15

The next day couldn't come fast enough. All night, I fantasized about seeing Blue's face. It was crazy the kind of effect he had on me. For hours while Damon was asleep, I sat up in bed watching Blue's music videos and interviews on YouTube. He had the #1 album in the country. I'd been listening to it non stop. It was soooo good.

Blue was a phenomenal rapper. He was dope as hell. I was completely enamored by him. Everything about him was on point. I knew I should've felt bad for fantasizing about another man when I was engaged but things between me and Damon were rocky as hell. Most days I didn't know if we were coming or going. Blue was my escape from my fucked up world. When I was around him all of my troubles melted away.

I'd picked out the perfect outfit for our rendezvous. My outfit matched the spring weather perfectly. I wore a chic brown silk shirt dress with the sleeved rolled up, a mini Louis Vuitton logo bag and brown gladiator open-toed boots. A gold chain link necklace and matching bracelet adorned my neck and wrist. I stepped out of my coupe and spotted Blue. He stood in front of the Philip Slein Gallery looking like a living piece of art.

There he was standing in front of the building puffing on a blunt. Smoke billowed from between his lips and evaporated into thin air. We were practically matching. Blue donned a white tee shirt, brown leather vest, mustard colored jeans and Tims. His beard was freshly lined and trimmed.

Oh how I loved a man with a beard. The shit looked good as hell on Blue. The sheer sight of him made my nipples hard. The swag and sex appeal he possessed should've been bottled up and contained. His waves were spinning. His biceps resembled mountain peaks and his tattoos well… I wanted to lick'em. Blue inhaled the last of the blunt, mashed it on the ground then greeted me with a hug.

"You trying to get fucked?" He hugged me tight, lifting me off the ground.

My panties became wet as I became lost in his embrace.

"Why you say that?" I giggled like a school girl.

"You know why." He put me down. "Yo' lil' hot ass wore this short ass shirt dress on purpose." Blue smacked my ass.

I prayed to god that nobody I or knew Damon was watching.

"Why did you wanna meet here?" I changed the subject.

"They're having a new art exhibit that I wanted to check out. Every time I come into town I stop here. It's one of my favorite art galleries. They carry the best art pieces. I want you to help me pick out something for my house." He led me inside.

Blue wasn't lying. Philip Slein was the shit. It was massive. The gallery had been open since 2008. Like most galleries all of the walls were painted white. The floors were made of wood. The current art exhibition was on an artist named Jamie Adams.

"I love Jamie Adams work." Blue said as we stood in front of one of his pieces. "From 2006 to 2012 he produced this series called the Jeannie Series. It's a series of black and white paintings based on the black and white Godard film, Breathless," he explained.

"Wow, I never knew you knew so much about art," I said, astonished.

"Just 'cause a nigga rap doesn't mean I don't know shit," Blue chuckled. "I ain't no dummy."

"I didn't say you were." I hit him playfully on the chest.

Blue's chest was rock solid. Goddamn this nigga is the truth.

"His artwork is beautiful." I said as we walked over to another piece.

"Yeah, I love it. That's why I gotta get a piece for the crib. So how have you been? I see that rock on your finger so you must be doing good." He lifted my hand.

I was praying he didn't notice my ring right off the bat. I had debated on whether or not I should wear it.

"You noticed that, huh?" I replied casually looking down at my hand.

"I see everything." Blue let my hand go.

Suddenly I became sad. I felt bad that Blue knew I was engaged. I didn't want to admit it but a part of me wished I was wearing his ring.

"What you lookin' all sad for?" Blue massaged my cheek with his thumb. "Somebody got to you before I could. It's all good. No hard feelings. I just hope you're happy."

I wanted desperately to say that I was but I honestly I couldn't. I was so fucked up emotionally it wasn't even funny. All Damon and I did was bicker and nitpick at each other. I wanted to believe him when he said that the only woman he loved was me but he'd said that before then turned around and broke my heart. His divorce to Isabel was still pending.

I had no support from anyone regarding our relationship except Tee-Tee. Even Dylan didn't like me and Damon being together. She felt that we were moving too fast but told me she'd support anything I decided to do. I honestly didn't know what I wanted. What was done was done. I couldn't rewind time and do it all over again. Damon and I were deep in the trenches together. I'd be a bitch if I turned my back on him now.

He'd given up his entire life for me. If that wasn't love I didn't know what was. Men aren't out here leaving ten year marriages on a whim. He had to be committed to making our relationship work. He said that he wasn't going to hurt me again. I had to believe him.

"I'm just glad you're not mad at me. I wanted to tell you but not over the phone."

"Who's the lucky man?" Blue placed his hands inside his pockets.

"His name is Damon. We were high school sweethearts."

"Go head on Cinderella. Look at you getting your happily ever after on," Blue joked.

"You silly." I looked down at my feet.

"Nah, for real." Blue placed his index finger under my chin and lifted my head up. "I'm happy for you. You deserve everything good that comes to you."

I didn't know if he was being politically correct or just masking his pain. Blue's facial expression rarely changed. Maybe I had been the only one feeling something between us this entire time.

"So have you been seeing anybody?" I probed.

I prayed to god he said no.

"Nah," Blue stopped and shook his head. "I've been too busy. Plus I thought… never mind." Blue resumed walking, letting his words linger in the air.

"You though what?" I stopped him.

"I thought me and you had something but obviously not."

My heart broke in a million pieces for. For the first time Blue had allowed his emotions to show on his face. He honestly looked disappointed that I was engaged. What had I done? Had I fucked up another relationship with someone I genuinely cared about? If Blue only knew how much I cared for him his feelings wouldn't be hurt. I liked him just as much as he liked me if not more. Hearing his voice alone brightened my day. But I'd already promised myself to another man. I had to let this thing with Damon play out or I'd wonder what if for the rest of my life. If Blue and I were meant to be we would be.

"Blue I care you a lot —" I began but he cut me off.

"Save your speech, lil' mama. It ain't even necessary. We good, like I said. I just want you to be happy." Blue played his true feelings off.

"So answer the question. Are you happy?"

I parted my lips and forced myself to say the word that I really didn't mean.

"Yes."

"That's all that matters then. C'mon lets get outta here." Blue placed his hand on the small of back and led me out.

"What happened to you buying a piece of artwork for your house?" I asked trying to keep up with him.

"I'm not in the mood anymore to buy artwork."

She just wanna run over my feelings, like she drinkin' and drivin'.

-Drake, "Connect"

Chapter 16

It had been three months since I'd last come to Sunday dinner. For whatever reason, my mother had decided to tuck her dick in-between her legs and call a truce. Maybe it was because it was her birthday that I was being welcomed back into the family fold. When my brother called to tell me the news, I played it off like it was no big deal but on the inside I was elated. I honestly missed being around my zany family. We were a strange dysfunctional bunch but they were my family and I wouldn't trade any of them for the world, including my mother. Damon was a little leery about going to Sunday dinner but came anyway to support me.

"I'm telling you now as soon as your mother gets to trippin' we are out." Damon announced pulling up into the driveway.

"I one hundred percent agree," I replied, checking my face in the mirror.

The party was a Garden of Eden theme. We all were requested to wear white. All of the ladies had to wear floral wreaths on their head. I wore mine. I thought I looked pretty but my mother would probably find something to gripe about.

Hand in hand Damon and I ventured into the backward. The sun was setting. It was 82 degrees so were having dinner outside. My mother's backyard was beautifully landscaped. It was designed for entertaining purposes. Lane's backyard was English inspired. Thousands of rare orchids and Amethyst Calla Lilies were planted everywhere. She also had a Olympic sized saltwater pool that sat next to a set of concrete benches.

For her birthday, my mother had a table set up underneath the covered wooden deck. Soft yellow light bulbs were mixed in with green foliage above everyone's heads. A table that sat ten was covered by a white linen table cloth. Peonies centerpieces, tea candles, green plates, wine glasses, pitchers of lemonade and Sangria decorated the able. The set up was absolutely breathtaking. The entire family including ZaShontay was out back sipping on cocktails and catching up.

"Here come Brangelina." My mother joked.

I knew my mother all too well. Her comment wasn't a joke it was her first dig of the night. Lane's snide remark wasn't worth replying to. I was more concerned with how she looked. She looked tired. Her skin seemed pale. She seemed out of it. She didn't look her normal vibrant self.

"Hello everyone," I waved.

"Hey baby girl." My father gave me a warm hug. "I miss you."

"I miss you too, daddy," I spoke choking up.

I really did miss my dad.

"Damon." My father extended his hand.

"Mr. Vasi it's good to see you." Damon shook his hand.

"I'm so glad you came sis," Tee-Tee pinched my cheek.

"It's her birthday. I wouldn't miss it for the world," I replied, truthfully.

My mother was mean and cruel but she was still my mother. Birthdays were special. I was happy that she'd reached another one.

"Everyone have a seat, please." My mother announced with a drink in her hand.

She sat at the head of the table as always. Once again she was wearing a wig except this one was short and blonde. It reminded me of Ellen DeGeneres hairstyle. I didn't know what my mother's fascination with wigs was all of a sudden but I really wished she would get over it. She looked horrible. The wigs aged her. What took the cake was that my mother couldn't let bygones be bygones. After months of not speaking, she didn't even bother saying hello to me. I wasn't going to let her childish behavior deter me from being polite.

"Hi mama," I spoke rubbing her back.

"Sunday," she responded cutting her eyes at me.

She acted like she didn't want me touch her. *Don't cuss her out Sunday,* I thought taking my seat.

"So how has everyone been?" I asked as Rosa and another maid brought out the first course.

We were having a chilled pea soup with bacon crumbled on top.

"Good," Dylan replied. "Angel's next fight is coming up so we're excited about that."

"I'm happy to hear that. Hopefully, I'll get an invite."

"Of course," Dylan assured.

After that no one said a word. You could cut the tension with a knife it was so thick. No one said a word. It was dead silent. All I heard was the sound of everyone slurping their soup and crickets buzzing. I'd never been more uncomfortable in my life. By the look on Damon's face he was feeling the same way.

"Mama, how is the Pink Hat's 40th anniversary party coming?" I tried to break the ice.

"It's coming along swimmingly. Isabel has been such a big help," she smirked, taking a drink from her glass.

Here she go. This chick just don't know when to quit.

"Speaking of Isabel how's the divorce coming, Damon?" My mother asked.

"Don't answer that," I told Damon. "She's only trying to start trouble."

"Let the man speak Sunday." My mother insisted.

"We're still working everything out," Damon answered, uncomfortable.

"So after your divorce is finalized are you and Sunday going to get married right away or are you going to wait a while?"

"We haven't really discussed that." I answered for Damon.

"Come on ya'll, its mama's birthday. Let's not fight," Tee-Tee said, flushing in distress.

"Nobody's fighting. We're having a pleasant conversation," My mother replied defensively. "Aren't we darling?" She winked her eye at me.

"Right," My father agreed. "We just want the best for baby girl. I personally don't think they should rush into marriage. They have all the time in the world to get

225

married. I suggest you two let the dust clear first then see where you're at a year or two from now."

"I agree Eric." My mother raised her glass. "That's about the smartest thing you've said in god knows how long. Maybe if you two wait a while it won't look so bad. I mean it's obvious that despite how we feel you're going to ruin your life, Sunday. I just hope this works out for you. I mean, I know it won't but when it does blows up in your face, we'll be here to pick you up as always."

"Ok mama," Tee-Tee interjected, dropping his spoon into his bowl. "That's enough. You swore you wouldn't start."

"No, let her finish," I urged. "I'm dying to hear what she has to say. Continue mama." My nostrils flared.

"I mean, let's not pretend like you're not ruining a family. Both of you are in the wrong but Damon is a man. A man is gonna be a man, we all know this but Sunday you know better. Well at least I thought you did. Is your self esteem so low that you'll just settle for anything? I mean for god sake have some dignity, girl" My mother finished off her drink.

"Rosa! Mama needs a refill," I yelled.

My mother glared at me and held out her cup for Rosa to fill it up. She was lit. Her words were slurring and she could barely sit up straight.

"How dare your drunk ass try to tell me anything," I shot seething with anger. "You can't give me relationship advice. Your own marriage didn't even work. Daddy ran out and got the youngest, dumbest THOT he could find just to get rid of the thought of you!"

"Aww shit! Now I gots to cut your daughter." ZaShontay pulled out a switch blade.

"Sunday don't bring ZaShontay into this." My father took up for her.

"Shut up daddy!" I shot.

I'd had it. No more biting my tongue. I was about to let their ass have it.

"You call me miserable?" I stood up and placed the palms of my hand on the table.

Leaning over I got in my mothers face.

"Look at you. You're a drunk. You look like shit. All you do is drink. A drunk can't tell me shit about my life."

"Sunday, stop. You're going to say something you're going to regret." Dylan pleaded, trying to make me sit back down.

"Stay out of this Dylan," I warned, flinging my arm free.

"Ya'll can continue to sugarcoat the shit if you want to but I'm not. She's a fuckin' drunk! All of my life she's treated me like shit! What the fuck have I ever done to you? You treat Tee-Tee like he's the greatest thing on earth and me like I'ma pain in your ass! What mother treats their child like that? And what makes it so bad is that ya'll have sat by and let her do it! Especially you daddy! You never took up for me," I cried. "None of you did. For once I'm going to do what makes me happy. I don't give a damn what ya'll got to say."

"Now look Sunday I know that you're upset but you're not going to disrespect me. I'm your father. All I'm doing is trying to help." My father said with a sudden fierceness.

"Well help yourself to someone your own age then get back to me." I said at once.

"Eric, don't waste your breath. She's a lost cause. If Sunday wants to look like a fool then let her. But when he hurts you and oh he's going to hurt don't come crying back to us." My mother made her feelings clear.

"I won't." I picked up my purse. "C'mon Damon," I snapped, storming off.

"Sunday wait!" Tee-Tee called after me.

"No! I'm tried of this shit! Fuck her!" I cried walking fast.

Tee-Tee caught up with me and took me into his arms.

"I'm sorry. I didn't expect for this to happen."

"I hate her," I wailed.

"Shhhhhh. You don't mean that." Tee-Tee rocked me from side to side.

But I did. I loved my mother dearly but hated her at the same time. Sadly, this was what my life had become, one fuckin' disaster after another. No matter how much I tried to be happy, life kept knocking me right back down. My mother had finally broken me. In my brothers arms I released 30 years of tears onto his shirt. I thought Isabel was my mortal enemy but really my mother was. I'd never felt a mother's love and probably never would. Lane hated me. I had to face it. She and I would never be close. I was a motherless child.

Niggas be on that bullshit.
Having us lookin' stupid.

-Sevyn Streeter, "B. A. N. S"

Chapter 17

For days after the showdown at my mother's house I cried. Damon, Tee-Tee, Emma and Dylan tried to console me but I was inconsolable. I was demolished. My parents had destroyed me. They made me wish that I was never born. Tee-Tee might as well have been an only child. After the blow up with my mom I was done. I was done with her and her bullshit ambush tactics.

I was done with my dad too. I was done with anybody that had anything negative to say about me or my relationship. I was moving forward with my life. I had a wedding to plan and babies to birth but first I had to get through the holiday. It was the 4th of July and Damon's daughters were coming over for the first time. I was excited and nervous at the same time.

It would be my first time meeting them. I didn't know if they'd hate or love me. I'd prayed about it all week. Now the day was here. It would be just us, the girls,

Emma and her family. I decorated the house with everything I could find that was red, white and blue. I bought balloons, beach balls for the pool, an American flag, streamers and more. Fireworks were illegal in St. Louis but I insisted that we have them. The 4th of July wasn't fun if you didn't have something to blow up.

I even went out and bought Barbie dolls and a karaoke machine for the girls to play with. Emma and her family had already arrived. Despite her feelings for Damon she wouldn't have missed our get together for the world. Besides, I needed the support. If Emma wouldn't have been there I would've most certainly been drunk by now. I was super afraid of meeting Damon's daughters. Our first encounter would define our relationship moving forward.

"How do I look?" I spun around and faced Emma.

She sat on the edge of Damon's bed with her legs crossed eating an apple.

"You look fine." She huffed leaning her head to the side.

Emma was over my dramatic behavior. I'd tried on five different outfits in the last thirty minutes. I wanted to be presentable yet fashion forward when I met the girls.

"I don't look like a slut do I?" I posed with my hands on my hips.

My hair was up in a chic bun. Since it was the 4th of the July I wanted a simplistic but sexy makeup look. I rocked a black cat eye, loads of mascara and M.A.C. Ruby Woo lipstick on my luscious lips. I wore a stars and stripes bikini with a white sarong tied around my waist.

"You do but what's new." Emma replied.

"I do?" I gasped.

"No," Emma giggled. "You look fine. I mean your massive boobs are a bit much in that bikini top but there is nothing you can do about that."

I looked down at my boobs. They looked almost pornographic.

"I was thinking that too. Maybe I'll ditch the sarong and wear this fishnet cover up." I slipped it on over my head.

"Much better." Emma gave me a thumbs up.

"You sure?" I questioned still slightly unsure.

"Yeeessss," Emma stressed. "The girls are gonna love you. It'll be fine. Trust me."

"Okay," I exhaled my worries.

"You have no idea how good it feels to be off mommy duty for the day," Emma gushed. "I told John to act like I was a dead beat dad and pretend I wasn't around."

"I can't stand you," I laughed.

"I'm serious. This girl right here," she pointed to her chest. "is about to have a few cocktails, kick back and get a sun tan."

"You know white folks ain't supposed to sun tan."

"This white girl here is. Give me all the skin cancer," Emma joked, cracking up.

"Emma!" I exclaimed.

"Just kidding. C'mon." She linked arms with me. "Let's go outside. I need a drink."

"Me too."

Emma and I didn't even make it all the way down the steps when the front door swung open. Damon was back from picking up the girls. His youngest daughter Milan raced through the door with her pink crab shape inflatable floatie. Milan was five years old and was the cutest little thing I'd ever seen. She looked like a mini version of Damon but was way cuter. Milan had the smoothest caramel skin, almond shaped eyes and afro puffed hair.

Damon's oldest daughter Gia slowly sauntered in after Milan. She walked in like she owned the place. Homegirl had a full on attitude. She had the same sour expression on her face that her mother wore. She was a beautiful little girl but seemed to be very sad and angry.

Gia was nine and was the spitting image of her mother. She was already 5'7 and had legs like a giraffe. Gia was going to be fighting boys off of her left and right. Damon was going to have his hands full with her.

"You're back." I skipped down the steps.

"Yeah," Damon replied with an attitude.

I didn't know what was wrong with him but he seemed pissed.

"Daddy, can I go get in the pool?" Milan jumped up and down eagerly.

"Not yet. Daddy has somebody he wants you to meet."

"You okay, babe?" I asked leaning forward to give him a light kiss on the cheek.

My lips didn't even get to connect with Damon's face. He snatched his head back and looked at me like I was crazy.

"Not in front of my kids." He scolded me.

"My bad," I responded shocked.

I had no idea that we had a no affection clause for when the girls came over.

"Ok, I'm uncomfortable." Emma rocked back and forth on her heels.

"Girls, say hello to Mrs. Hunter," Damon said.

"Hi," Milan waved.

Gia just stood there looking up at the ceiling annoyed.

"Hello girls," Emma spoke back. "Wow Damon, they have gotten so big since the last time I saw them."

"Can I go watch television?" Gia asked dryly.

"No we talked about this in the car. You're going to join us outside," Damon fumed.

"I don't wanna go outside wit' ya'll. It's too hot. I don't even wanna be here!" Gia stomped her foot.

"You made that clear on the car ride over here and I told you that we were going to spend the holiday together as a family."

"She ain't none of my damn family." Gia cut her eyes at me.

"What I have I told you about cursing? You ain't grown!" Damon pointed his finger in Gia's face like a gun.

"Somebody needs an ass whooping," I whispered to Emma.

"You got that right," she replied.

"Now apologize to Mrs. Vasi," Damon demanded.

Gia groaned and reluctantly spat, "Sorry."

"It's ok sweetie." I shot Gia a fake smile.

"Milan and Gia say hi to my good friend Mrs. Vasi." Damon introduced us.

Friend? Since when had I become just his friend? I wasn't his friend last night when he had his dick in my mouth. I thought I was his damn fiancée?

"Hi." Milan shyly hid behind her father.

"Hi girls. You ready to celebrate?" I asked cheerfully.

"Yes!" Milan stepped from behind her dad. "Daddy can we please go get in the pool now?"

"Yes bubble butt. We can go get in the pool now." Damon took Milan's little hand in his and led her outdoors.

Gia followed behind them looking like she wanted nothing more than to slit her wrist.

"What was that shit about?" Emma asked when the coast was clear.

239

"Your guess is just as good as mine. Maybe he hasn't told the girls that we're engaged yet."

"Oh Gia knows something is up," Emma countered.

"Yeah, she does," I agreed.

"You still wanna be a step-mama?" Emma teased me.

"Not if I gotta deal with Gia's bad ass on a regular basis."

"I told you it wouldn't be easy. C'mon step mama." Emma dragged me outdoors.

By the time we got outside Damon and Milan had joined Emma's husband and their two boys in the pools. Baby Jada was sound asleep in her pumpkin seat. The sun was beaming down on us but a cool breeze kept everyone from sweating to death. Emma and I stripped down to our bathing suits and lie down on the cushioned outdoor chaise lounge. We lathered our bodies with SPF sunscreen and allowed the sun to do its magic.

Damon and John played with the kids. They had a game of Marco Polo going on. I loved seeing Damon interact with Milan. He was such a good father. The love for his girls showed all over his face. While we all enjoyed the holiday the chef hired for the day barbequed meat on the grill.

Gia lay next to me with her Beats By Dre headphones over her ears. The angry scowl on her face was still there. I thought maybe if I tried to talk to her she would feel better so I tapped her on the leg to get her attention. Gia pretended like she didn't feel me touch her. My ignorant ass tapped her lil' grown butt again. This time she responded.

"What?" She pulled her headphones from off her ears.

"Are you hungry 'cause I can have the chef make you a burger or something until we eat dinner." I tried to be nice.

"If I was hungry I'd tell my dad. Now leave me alone." Gia rolled her eyes at me.

Jesus be a fence. I don't wanna slap her.

"So what grade are you in?" I asked politely, hoping Gia would chill.

241

"None of your business." She rolled her eyes.

"Do you get whoopings?" I asked, curious.

"Sunday, you can't ask that child that?" Emma tried her best not to laugh.

"Why the hell not? She grown enough to talk slick, she's old enough to get beat."

"My daddy wouldn't dare spank me. I'm his little princess," Gia beamed. "He loves me and my mommy with all of his heart. He tells us it all the time."

"I'm sure he does." I rolled my eyes thinking she was talking shit.

This lil' girl was obviously on one. She knew that Damon and I were together. She was obviously team Isabel and Damon and I could respect that. Who wouldn't want their parent's to be together but Gia would have to accept the fact that her father and I were in a relationship now.

"I love my daddy so much and he loves me. He loves our family. My mommy said that this little faze he's going through will end soon. He'll be back home with us eventually."

"If you say so Chucky," I yawned not fazed by her little speech.

Stop it Sunday. She's just a kid. She doesn't know any better. Just try to be nice.

"Look Gia." I turned and lay on my side to face her. "It's apparent that you know I'm not just your father's friend. We're engaged to be married and I'm going to be in your life. Hopefully, you can accept that 'cause I really would like to get to know you better."

"Well, I don't want to get to know you." Gia rolled her neck. "I have a mother. Her name is Isabel McKnight."

"This child is 9 going on 30," I said, ready to strangle her.

"Sorry to bust ya' bubble Wednesday but my mommy and daddy are getting back together so accept that."

"Let me tell you something demon seed." I sat up. "I don't play with other peoples kids. I will beat the breaks off yo' lil' ass."

"Old lady, you ain't gon' touch me 'cause if you do my daddy will murder you. Don't be mad at me 'cause he still loves my mommy."

"Ok Angelica, go back to listening to your music. I'm done talkin' to you. If you wanna pretend like yo' daddy still loves your mother, go head. Have at it." I waved Gia off and lie back down.

I was not about to sit up and argue with a 9 year old. I was over trying to connect with her lil' bad ass. I had no time for disrespectful, smart mouth, little girls.

"My daddy does too still love my mother," Gia shot adamantly. "They go to marriage counseling every Tuesday and Thursday."

"What?" My head whipped around in her direction.

"Oh you didn't know that, did you?" Gia sneered. "Now who looks like the dummy?" She interlocked her fingers and placed them behind her head, pleased with herself.

The devil is a liar. Gia had to be lying. There was no way that Damon was attending marriage counseling sessions with Isabel. Then I remembered that on Tuesday

244

and Thursdays Damon claimed he had to work late. He wouldn't come home on those nights until almost midnight. Holy shit! I'm about to kill him.

"Calm down Sunday," Emma urged.

She knew I was seething with anger.

"No fuck that! Damon!" I called out his name.

"Yeah?" He stopped playing with the kids.

"In the house now!" I stomped my way indoors.

I was so mad, I felt all the blood rush to my head. Damon came inside with a towel wrapped around his waist. He found me pacing back and forth in the living room.

"What's wrong wit' you?"

"You lied to me." I continued to pace the room.

"Lied to you about what, Sunday?" What have I lied to you about now?" He asked visibly annoyed.

"What exactly do you do when you work late on Tuesdays and Thursdays?" I stopped and glared at him.

"I told you I have to sign off on a lot of paperwork." He looked away. "Why?"

"It's so easy for you to sit up here and lie to my face. Am I that gullible to you?" I iced grilled him.

"Actually, I'm not sitting, I'm standing up and once again I have no idea what you're talkin' about." Damon tried to play me off like I was crazy.

"Yo' black ass don't be working late. On Tuesdays and Thursdays you're attending marriage counseling sessions with Isabel! Now look my in the face and tell me I'm lying!"

"Who told you that?" His eyes grew wide.

"Yo' big head daughter!" I mushed him in the forehead.

"Don't put your hands on me no more Sunday." Damon warned smacking my hand away.

"Boy please, ain't nobody scared of you." I looked him up and down like he wasn't shit.

"Instead of smacking my hand away you need to beat the brakes off yo' lil' fast ass daughter but that's none

246

of my business. I'm just your friend." I spat sarcastically, making air quotes with my hand. "So when were you going to tell me that you were having second thoughts about us?"

"I just want to make sure that I'm making the right decision. Isabel and I have kids together. We got history. I just can't pick up and divorce her like that." Damon tried to explain.

"Umm excuse you but you should've thought about all of that before you proposed to me!"

"I know but we've just been arguing a lot. You been sad and shit. It's just too much."

"So now this is my fault?" I questioned about to flip.

"Did I say that?" Damon mean-mugged me. "There you go putting words in my mouth! This why I can't fuckin' talk to you. You always making something about you. Life doesn't revolve around you, Sunday. I got other people I need to take into consideration."

"Who? Isabel? Just admit it. You still love her."

247

"Man gon' wit' that. " He waved me off. "I love you. You know that."

"I don't know shit but that you're fuckin' a liar. Have you been fuckin' her this whole time?" I got up in his face. "Did you fuck her on Valentines Day?"

"No! I already told you that. Don't ask me that shit no more!" Damon walked away from me and sat down on the back of the couch.

"And I'm really supposed to believe you after finding out you've been lying to me? You still love her. That's why your so called divorce hasn't gone through yet. Hell, is there even a divorce?"

"I'm not gon' answer that." Damon hung his head agitated by my line of questioning.

"I ain't seen no paperwork. If you're getting a divorce then why are you going to marriage counseling with her? The shit don't add up!"

"We're trying to make sure that we're doing the right thing."

"You know what," I said, fed up.

"You two confused muthafucka's can kiss my black ass. Let me do you both a favor so this can be an easier decision for you." I pulled my engagement ring off my finger.

"Go work shit out wit' your wife. I'm done fuckin' wit' you." I let the ring fall to the floor and ran upstairs.

"Sunday wait!" Damon called after me.

I didn't bother to stop. There was nothing else to say and I refused to let him see me cry. He'd lied to me repeatedly. He'd led me on. He'd made a fool out of me just like my mother said he would. He didn't care about me. If he did he would've never treated me this way. Our so called relationship was a farce. Damon and I were over and this time there would be no going back.

When you need to smile but you can't afford it.

-Emelie Sande, "Breaking The Law"

Chapter 18

Alone, I lay in my bed staring blankly at the ceiling. I'd been doing this for weeks. Sleeping and staring at the ceiling had become my daily routine. I'd completely shut myself off from the world. I didn't wanna hear a bunch of lousy ass I told you so's. I already felt dumb enough. I just hated that my mother was right. Why the fuck did she have to be right? I so wanted to prove her wrong. Everything she'd said about Damon was true. He'd broken my heart and left me for dead.

I couldn't do shit but stare at the ceiling and cry myself to sleep. I needed my happy back. I was so tired of being played by men. Damon was supposed to be different. He was supposed to be the answer to all of my problems but he'd quickly morphed into my opponent. When he told me he loved me I believed him. I could see it in his eyes. I could feel it in his touch. I felt it in his stroke. Nothing about our love was a lie.

What was a lie was how much he loved me. A man that truly loved a woman would never betray her trust. Damon had betrayed my trust not once but twice. I couldn't keep on giving him chances to break my heart. But letting him go wasn't so easy. It was painful as fuck. Waking up alone knowing he wasn't by my side was gut-wrenching. I physically felt sick every minute of the day.

I wanted to rip my insides out. It seemed like the pain got worse with each day. I couldn't take it. Being lovesick was the absolute worse. Damn had called me a million times trying to apologize. He'd even attempted to come by and talk things out but I was determined to stay strong. I had to figure this shit out on my own without Damon's influence.

Loving a nigga will make you do stupid shit and here I was feeling like the ultimate fool. I'd almost had my happily after. I was moments away from walking down the aisle. Now here I was back at square one. It wasn't fair. How come everybody else got to be madly in-love? I wanted the man, the sick house and kids. Hell, I deserved my knight and shining armor and picket fence so why couldn't I achieve it? Was I giving my heart to the wrong man? When I lay in Damon's arms at night it felt right but when we faced the world it felt like everyone was against us.

Here I was thinking all of these years that I was his long lost love that got away. Maybe I was never as special to Damon as I thought. Maybe all of the years I had been playing second fiddle to Isabel. Maybe she was the love of his life. The mere thought of Damon loving Isabel more than he loved me made me want to vomit.

I lay underneath my white down comforter and looked to my left where he used to lay. The scent of Damon's cologne still lingered in my sheets. Goddamn, I wanna call him. Maybe enough time had passed. Maybe I should hear him out. Maybe it was all one big understanding. Maybe I'd overreacted. Instead of yelling and cursing I should've listened when he tried to explain his self.

Missing him terribly, I reached over and grabbed his pillow. I inhaled his intoxicating scent and felt myself die a slow death all over again. I had to hear his voice. One phone call wouldn't hurt. A rush of adrenaline washed over my body as I picked up my phone to give him a call.

Searching through my call log I found his number. I was just about to press my index finger against his name when I was stopped by the sound of my doorbell. Now was not the time for unexpected guests. I wasn't in the mood for it. I lay quiet, barely breathing; praying whoever was at my door would go away. They didn't.

"Sunday! Open up! It's me Dylan!" She banged her fist against my door.

"God," I groaned, getting out of the bed.

Mad as hell I stomped towards the door and opened it.

"Girl, we have been calling you for days." Dylan barged in with my Aunt Candy not too far behind her.

My Aunt Candy was a trip. She was 54 years old but acted like she was 21. You couldn't tell my Aunt Candy she wasn't the shit. She had a bad body to be an old doll. I just wished she'd dress her age. It was a regular ole Wednesday afternoon and she rocked a bright neon yellow half sleeve, crop top, cut-out, knee length skirt and her favorite stripper heels. My eyes were simply not ready.

"We thought yo' behind was over here dead," Candy said. "You know how chicks like to kill they self over niggas these days."

"As you can see I'm fine. I'm not on suicide watch so you two can leave." I held the door open for them.

"We're not going anyway. You need us right now and we're going to be here for you." Dylan made me sit down next to her on the couch. "How are you feeling, cousin. Are you okay?"

"No," I responded wanting to die.

"You young girls gon' learn to quit giving your heart to these niggas. Didn't Chris Brown tell you these hoes ain't loyal?" Candy crossed her legs.

"You should've known his ass was no good when he proposed to you while still being married to his old bitch. Where they do that at? Damon's ass was trying to set ya'll up to be on some damn sister wives shit. Listen to what ya' aunty tellin' you." She lit a cigarette.

"Can I smoke in here? Ok, thank you." Candy said not bothering to wait for a response.

"All I want to know is how do I stop loving him aunty? I've been in-love with him since we were kids," I asked, praying she'd have the answer.

"Girl, love ain't real," Candy flicked her wrist dismissively. "That shit is just an imaginary feeling you young girls trick yourself into believing in. You gots to have a heart of steel with these men."

"Like you and my mama?" I remarked. "Ya'll don't feel a thing."

Candy hung her head and laughed.

"Your mama is more soft and pink then you think. She just pretends to be tough. That's why she don't like me 'cause she knows I'm the real deal."

"When are you two going to make up?" Dylan quizzed.

"When she get over old shit," Candy declared, indignantly. "I don't know if I ever told you the story but Lane is mad at me 'cause I stole Dylan's daddy from her."

"What?!" Dylan screeched.

"Yeah, he and Lane had a little thing going on but it was nothing serious. He took her out on a few dates, bought her some ice cream and a diamond necklace or two and she thought they were an item."

"It sounds like they were, mama." Dylan replied, sternly.

"Ok maybe they were but ya' daddy always had eyes for me. Lane just got to him before I could."

"So you stole my daddy away from Aunt Lane?" Dylan said in disbelief.

"It ain't stealing if the nigga came willingly." Candy corrected Dylan.

"Me and Lane fought behind that shit. I beat her monkey ass. She was my little sister. She ain't know how to handle no man like Dylan's daddy."

"Candy you were wrong as hell for that." Dylan tuned up her face.

"Yeah, I was. Your father was her first lil' love but it's been over thirty years. The girl gots to get over it."

"So that's why my mama was going so hard about me being with Damon. She felt like I was doing to Isabel what you had done to her." I spoke having an Oprah ah ha moment.

"Yeah, your mother loved Dylan's father. She couldn't bare seeing us together but she loved her niece. I always thought that maybe deep down she always wished that Dylan was hers."

"That would explain why she hates me so much." I said feeling depressed all over again.

"Lane doesn't hate you. She just sees so much of herself in you that it scares her. You're soft and pink just like your mama. When Lane loves, she loves hard just like you. She only wants the best for you. She just doesn't know how to show it. Go a little easy on her. She means well, she does."

"Well she's got a pretty shitty way of showing it," I quipped.

"I know she does. Hell, me and Dylan went through the same thing but we're better now. We understand each other more now. You have to understand Sunday. Me and ya mama weren't raised to be all lovey dovey. Your grandmother Dahl was no joke. She was a tough woman but she loved yo' mama. Lane was her favorite. She treated me like the ugly stepchild."

"That's how my mama treats me. She adores Tee-Tee. He can do no wrong in her eyes."

"That ain't right but you know we're old. It's hard to break old folk from their ways. I'm sure you and Lane will figure it out. You got time. When you're feeling better, call her and try to talk it out. But in the meantime," Candy took a long pull from her cigarette.

"Ain't no need for you to be sitting over here looking all ugly and shit. I can bet you fifty dollars that nigga ain't sitting over there sad. You betta get up, paint yo' face, do yo' hair and throw on something tight. Remember, in order to get over one man you gotta get under a new one. You betta get up and get yo' back cracked, girl."

My Aunt Candy had a point. Sitting around being sad and miserable was only making me feel worse. Isolating myself wasn't working either. I was only hurting myself. Damon and I had tried and failed. Well more like he'd fucked me over. He'd built me up to only let me down. Fuck Damon! His lying, unsure ass could kiss my behind. Aunt Candy's advice was golden. It was time for me to get over Damon McKnight by getting under someone new and I had just the perfect guy in mind.

I know we only fuckin' outta spit
'cause ya' man don't do you
right.

~Drake, "Wu-Tang Forever"

Chapter 19

I must be out of my fuckin' mind. I have officially gone crazy. After my Aunt Candy's speech, I hit up Blue. He was thrilled to hear from me. I was overjoyed to talk to him. He was in New York doing a three night show at the Barclay Center. It would be weeks before he was back in St. Louis. I couldn't wait that long to see him so I decided to hop on a plane to New York.

Blue had no idea that I was coming. I hoped he didn't think I was some crazy lunatic for showing up unannounced. I had to take a leap of faith and put myself out there to him. Since I'd known Blue he'd made it his business to show me how much he was feeling me. It was high time I show him what he meant to me. I had a huge surprise for him.

It was dark by the time I landed in New York City. I checked into my room at the St. Regis hotel. Blue normally got back to his hotel room by midnight. I had just enough time to shower and dress. The doll had to look good for ya' boy. I put on something extra chic for Blue. I felt ultra sexy in my black findersKEEPERS time travelers dress. The dress was sleeveless with a dramatic ruffled hem. I wore my hair flat ironed straight to the back. A pair of black Giuseppe Zanotti multi strapped buckled booties completed the look.

It was a simplistic yet highly edgy ensemble. Blue was sure to like it. At least I hoped. With my gift in hand I had my driver whisk me away to Blue's hotel. He was staying at the Trump Soho New York. On the ride over it dawned on me. What if I showed up and Blue had a chick with him? Better yet what if he had several chicks with him? I know how rappers do. They have their security guards scope out chicks during the show to bring back to the hotel.

After the show was the after party and rappers like Blue had to turn up. I just hoped I didn't turn up and ruin the turn up. I also didn't want to get my feelings hurt. I'd been through enough over the past few weeks. My poor heart couldn't withstand anymore pain.

I was already here so there was no turning back now. The driver pulled up in front of the hotel. I inhaled deep and tried to control my anxiety. Suddenly, I'd become nervous as hell. I'd had balls of steel on the flight. Somewhere between the plane ride and now I'd lost it. It was time to woman up and put my big girl panties on. If Blue was some other shit it was best I find out now instead of later.

My driver helped me out of the back seat of the car and handed me Blue's present. Blue's gift was huge. The doorman held the door open for me as I walked inside the hotel. I quickly boarded the elevator. Holding Blue's gift was making my arms hurt. I rode the elevator all the way to the penthouse on the 43rd floor.

Blue had mentioned to me that was where he was staying. Little did I know but when I got to his floor two big burley body guards were waiting there. They reminded me of two skyscrapers, they were so tall. Each of them wore all black. The guards had to be almost 400 pounds each. Neither of them smiled at me. They both looked at me with disdain, like I was some chicken head groupie.

"You gotta go sweetheart." The guard on the right shooed me away.

"I'm here to see Blue. My name is Sunday. He knows me."

"Sure he does and I know Janet Jackson." The guard chuckled.

"I'm telling the truth. I really do know him. Can you tell him Sunday is here?" I cranked my neck back to look at him.

"If Blue were expecting you, your name would be on the list. I don't see no Sunday on the list. Do you see a Sunday on the list, Joe?"

"Nope and a Monday either. What kind of name is Sunday anyway? Your parents had to be getting high to name you after a day of the week," Joe joned.

Oh so these fat muthafucka's got jokes?

"I will fight yo' big ass." I warned knowing damn well I would get my ass kicked. "Can you do your job and let Blue know I'm here." I snapped fed up.

"I can't hold this any longer," I said struggling with Blue's present.

"You need to go." Joe pressed the down button on the elevator and tried to push me onto it.

"You better get yo' damn hands off of me!" I yanked away.

"Give it up Thursday. Don't embarrass yourself." Joe tried to grab me but I dodged him.

I dipped past him with the quickness almost dropping Blue's gift in the process. I swear my heart stopped beating for a second. Blue's gift had cost me a kidney. If this Biggie Small looking muthafucka made me break it I was going to kill him.

"Blue!" I yelled.

"We don't want to have to hurt you." Joe and I faced off.

"Fuck you! Blue!" I called out again.

Lord please, let this man hear me.

"Blue!"

"Lady, don't make me restrain you." The other guard warned.

"You need to restrain from eating so goddamn much. How about that?" I quipped.

"Alright, that did it." Joe lunged at me but once again I was too quick.

In 4 inch heels, I was shaking his ass like Allen Iverson in his prime. It looked like me and the guards were playing a game of touch football as I dodged their attempts at capturing me.

"Bluuuuuuuuuee!" I shouted even louder.

I was damn near out of breath by the time he opened the door. Blue stepped out into the hall with a surprised look on his face.

"What's going on?"

"This chick is crazy." Joe huffed and puffed.

"Blue... thank god you're here." I panted out of breath too. "The M&M twins didn't believe that I knew you."

"She's good fellas. Let her through," Blue laughed. "When did you get here?" He greeted me with a warm hug.

"Today. I came just to see you. Are you surprised?" I inhaled his scent.

He was wearing the most enthralling cologne I'd ever had the pleasure of smelling. Blue's big ass looked good enough to eat. He was dressed simply in all black. He wore an all black tee shirt, jeans and socks.

"Yeah, lil' crazy girl. C'mon." He escorted me inside his suite.

"I told you I knew him!" I spat to the guards, sticking out my tongue.

The inside of Blue's penthouse suite was magnificent. It was 1,800 square feet. It had an entry foyer, full service breakfast bar and wet bar, dining area and two bedrooms. Blue had the entire floor to his self. Like I'd expected there were chicks and a gang of dudes in his room. It was five dudes and eight girls so I wondered who was there for Blue.

Why did I bring my ass up here? I should've stayed my ass in St. Louis. What the fuck was I thinking? I am so fuckin' stupid. Blue had a whole kick back in full swing. They were vibing out to music, drinking and playing beer pong. I felt like such an intruder. The scantily clad women were giving me the stank eye. It was time for me to go before I fucked up a bitch.

"Why didn't you tell me you were coming? I wouldn't have had all these people here," Blue confirmed.

"I wanted to surprise you. I hope I'm not overstepping my boundaries by just showing up." I looked around nervously.

"You know better than that. I'm happy as fuck to see you." He hugged me again. "You can surprise me anytime."

"Good," I blushed. "Here, I bought you this." I passed him his gift.

"What is this?" Blue eyed me suspiciously.

"Just open it." I smiled hard.

Blue ripped the wrapping off it and found the Jamie Adams piece he'd been eyeing that day we were at the art gallery.

"Yo… you didn't." He said astonished.

"You like it?" I asked anxiously.

"You know I do. Damn." He leaned the painting up against the wall and stepped back to get a better look at it. "This is the dopest thing anybody has ever done for me. Thank you." Blue pulled me close and kissed me on the lips.

"Yo my bad." He stepped back quickly, catching his self. "I forgot you're engaged."

"Wrong. She's single." I held up my bare left hand.

"Word?"

"Yeah."

"I'm not sorry to hear that but we'll get off into that in a minute. Let me introduce you to my people."

Blue introduced me to everyone. I said hello.

"You hungry or thirsty?" He asked.

"Nah, I'm good," I assured.

"Thank you again for the painting. I still can't believe you did that."

"You're welcome. You deserve it."

"C'mon lets go upstairs." He picked up a bottle of Jack Daniels whisky and led me upstairs.

Seeing the bottle reminded me of my mother. I followed Blue up the stairs to his room that led out to the rooftop pool. The stars shined bright above us. The water in the pool was turquoise blue. Blue and I stood by it. His right arm was wrapped around my shoulder. He took a few sips from the bottle then handed it to me. I took a swig. The whisky burned my throat and warmed my insides.

"I'm glad you came to come see me. When I get some time off you gon' have to help me decorate my crib." He looked up at the sky.

The sky was pitch black. We were so high up I swore I could touch the stars.

"I'm down," I agreed.

"You fine as fuck. You know that?"

Blue stared at me with his hazel eyes and I melted. My god this man is a blessing.

"You're not too bad yourself," I grinned.

"So what happened between you and ole' boy?" Blue placed the bottle of Jack down on the ground.

"It's a long story but to make a long story short he was married when he proposed to me."

"Oh that's how you get down?" He drew his head back.

"No!" I exclaimed. "He and his wife were separated when we got back together. They were getting a divorce but he started having second thoughts so I dipped."

"You make it seem so simple." Blue took his arm from around my shoulder and turned his back towards the pool. "Leaving him couldn't have been that easy. Wasn't he your high school sweetheart or some shit?"

"Yeah. We have a long history together and I loved him a lot but we're not meant to be." I convinced myself.

"So what I'm yo rebound nigga?"

"No!" I pushed him playfully.

But I pushed Blue too hard though. He flew back into the pool and took me right along with him. Our bodies crashed into the water. Thank god it was a heated pool or we would've been freezing. Blue and I both came up for air.

"Oh my god! I am so sorry!" I laughed, wiping my face.

"If you wanted to take a swim that was all you had to say." Blue grinned, swimming over to the side of the pool.

I swam over to him and wrapped my arms around his neck. The soft lights from the pool danced across our skin. I couldn't take it anymore. I had to taste him. Water dripped from my face as I placed my nose up against his. Blue palmed my ass. I slid my hands down his abs. For a minute we just floated there anticipating who was going to make the first move. His lips were inches away from mine.

"You sure you wanna do this?" He asked.

I was so enthralled in him all I could do was nod my head. Blue ran his fingers through the back of hair and pulled my face close to his. Our lips touched and magic was created. I wrapped my legs around his waist. His shirt had floated up so I pulled it off. Blue unbuckled his jeans. I wore no panties so there were none to take off. Within seconds his dick was inside me. I screamed out to the heavens. Blue was hitting me with the death stroke.

Each stroke filled me up. I was lost in his deep stroke. This was the moment I'd been waiting for. Day dreaming about making love to Blue didn't compare to the actual thing. This was a different form of bliss. The warm water waded back and forth as he gripped my ass and drove himself deeper inside of me.

Tears came to my eyes. I could barely breathe. Blue gazed into my eyes. I looked back into his. No words were spoken. Only erotic moans filled the atmosphere. We were connecting on a deeper level that only he and I could understand. Then we dove under water and made love. Our bodies floated as he fucked me in 10 feet of water. I could feel an orgasm near but I didn't want the moment to end. He felt too good inside of me.

Blue was taking me to the moon. I rode his spaceship to Mars. I could feel the stars as his tongue flickered against my neck. I held onto his back and allowed myself to be transported to outer space. Our rhythm was increasing but the second. Blue's dick was like a Congo drum. I didn't want the beat to come to an end. But all good things had to come to an end. There underneath the stars, the moon and god Blue and I created our own little slice of heaven.

All I need is a glass of you.
-KeKe Wyatt, "Lie Under
You"

Chapter 20

Blue and I had been rockin' for a month and a half. So far it was the best month and a half of my life. Since I'd surprised him in New York, I hadn't left his side. I'd traveled with Blue all over the world. We'd gone to London, Australia and Tokyo. I got to see him rehearse, perform, meet with his adoring fans and record.

Being with Blue was absolutely the best. I got to travel and spend quality time with my man. Yes, you read right. Blue was my man and I was his girl. When he wasn't working, he spent all of his time with me. We watched movies, went shopping, and visited art museums. I got Blue to read some of my favorite books and watch some of my favorite reality shows. He now was an avid watcher and fan of Love and Hip Hop Atlanta.

The Puerto Rican princess, Joseline Hernandez and Stevie J were his favorite characters. While on the road we played cards, chess and checkers. At night before going to bed I sang him to sleep, although I couldn't sing a lick. Blue didn't mind though. He said it was the only he could go to sleep now. I never thought it would be humanly possible to fall in-love with someone so fast but I loved Blue with all of my heart.

He treated me like a queen and I treated him like a king. He was by far my favorite person to be around. It was like we were kindred spirits. We spoke our own language. Nothing about being with him was complicated or drama-filled. Everything about us was easy. The peace I'd been seeking was finally found. I was actually living out my happily after ever.

Blue and I wanted the same things out of life. We had the same views on marriage, kids and our careers. I explained to him how soon I would have to return to the real world and get my career back on track. Blue understood. He encouraged me to follow my dreams. It was refreshing to meet a man that supported my aspirations.

Blue got to see the good, the bad and the ugly side of me. He quickly realized that I wasn't a morning person and that I snore in my sleep. He didn't mind when I didn't wear makeup. My hair didn't have to always be done and I didn't have to be the flyest bitch in the room all the time. He liked me just as I was. I was perfect in his eyes and he was perfect in mine.

Blue was loving. He was gentle and commanding. The man kept me on my toes. No two days with him were the same. I never wanted to return to St. Louis. Everything broken in my life was there and I didn't want to return home to it.

It was Labor Day weekend. We were at the Anjunbeats Pool Party in Miami turning up. Blue was hosting the event. Hundreds of people were there. The setting couldn't have been more perfect. I'd never seen anything like it. The party was being held at the Raleigh hotel. DJ Khaled was on the ones and twos. Everyone was going hard in the paint. Drinks were flowing. Hands were in the air. Nobody was sitting down.

Everyone was up dancing and having a good time. All types of music were being played from hip hop to techno. I lost my shit when DJ Khaled started playing New Orleans bounce music. I swear I had never had so much fun in my life. I was grooving shaking my ass to the beat. The sun, palm trees and ocean was my back drop.

I was standing in the V.I.P. section having a ball. I'd had three Mojito's so I was feeling nice. I was looking even better in my Mint Swim 'Rachel' skimpy bikini. The top was like any other classic bikini top but the bottoms were v shaped with cut-outs. Blue couldn't keep his hands off me. I loved all of the attention I was getting from him.

In a setting filled with hundreds of beautiful exotic women he only had eyes for me. There were tons of fine dudes there too but Blue was the only I could see. He wore no shirt. His muscles were out of control and the imprint of his dick in his shorts made me want to ride his dick until the sun came up.

Blue commanded the crowd with a bottle of Ciroc in his hand. He took the bottle to the head as he and his pot'nahs turned up. I stood off to the side admiring my boo. I was so happy he was mine. I was by far the luckiest girl in the world. Blue's smash hit *Down 4 Me* played. I swayed my thick hips to the beat. The song had a down south, chopped and screwed vibe to it. Whenever it came on I completely zoned out.

Blue spotted me grooving. He walked over and stood behind me. His hard dick was pressed in-between my ass cheeks. If this nigga didn't stop I was sure to fuck him in front of the crowd of people. Blue held me in his strong arms while he rapped into the microphone. All eyes were on us. Blue and I swayed to the beat. I wondered if he knew how much I adored him.

As the song went off, Blue kissed me on the back of my head. He handed the microphone to one of his mans and spun me around to face him. He didn't care who was watching. He kissed me long and hard in front of everyone. I hated being the center of attention but everyone around us had disappeared. All I could concentrate on was the taste of his sweet tongue.

"I can't wait to get you back to the room." I said, coming up for air.

"I'ma fuck the shit outta you." Blue grabbed a handful of my ass.

"Promise." I flicked my tongue across the lobe of his ear.

"Fuck that, we're about to head back to the room now." Blue said, seriously.

"Are you for real?" I asked astonished.

"Does it look like I'm playing? Look how hard my dick is." Blue pointed down to his package.

I gazed down and sure enough Blue was rock hard. My mouth instantly watered.

"Let's go." I said, eagerly.

"Let me tell my peoples we'll back real quick."

"Okay."

I watched Blue walk off. While I waited for his return, I reached into my pocket and pulled out my cell phone. I had twelve missed calls from Tee-Tee and five missed calls from Dylan. I didn't hesitate to call Tee-Tee back. Something had to be wrong for him to call me back to back. The phone barely rang once before he picked up.

"Why haven't you ain't been answering your phone?" He asked instead of saying hello.

""Cause I'm at a pool party. I couldn't hear my phone ring. What's up?"

"You gotta hurry up and come home." Tee-Tee said out of breath.

"Why?"

"Sunday, I really don't wanna tell you this over the phone." Tee-Tee began to cry.

"Tell me what?" I panicked.

My brother never cried. Something crazy must've happened.

"Is everybody ok?" My heart thumped in my chest.

"No... mama's dead."

Would you think a nigga rude if I said I wanna fuck right now?

~Trey Songz, "Don't Judge"

Chapter 21

My mother was dead. Dead. She was gone. I'd never see her face again, hear her voice or hear the clink of her glass as she drank Jack Daniels again. We'd never argue again. She'd never make another snide remark about my looks or my life. I should've been relieved but I wasn't. I felt like I'd been shot point blank in the face with a sawed off shot gun. On the plane ride home I kept telling myself that it was all a mistake. I'd get home and the whole entire thing would be a cruel joke but it wasn't.

I'd just finished watching my mothers casket drop into the ground. I wanted to jump in her grave and go with her but I couldn't. I was still physically alive but I felt dead on the inside. Nothing mattered to me anymore. Now that my mama was gone I was mentally fucked. My mother was only 51 years old. She was too young to die.

That evil bitch named breast cancer had taken her. It all made sense when I learned the news. My mother had breast cancer and the only person who knew was her doctor. She didn't tell anybody, not even ever her precious son Tee-Tee. Knowing my mother, she probably didn't want some pity party. My mother never liked showing too much affection or weakness. She had to go out like a G.

I kind of respected her decision to keep her illness a secret but resented it as well. We all could've been there for her. I know she had to have been scared. I know I would have been. There was no way that I could go through chemo treatments alone. My mothers' doctor revealed to us that a few months back the cancer had spread throughout her body.

The cancer had gotten so bad it was untreatable. My mother knew she only had a short time left to live. On the day she passed my mother had gone up to her room for a nap but never woke back up. When she didn't come down for dinner, Rosa went up to wake her but she'd already passed on. I was thankful that she'd died in her sleep. Nobody wants to die while awake.

I know I don't. I just hated that I hadn't spoken to her since her birthday. I'd thought about calling her several times but like always my pride got in the way. I always felt like she was the mother. It was her job to make things right with me but Lane never did. She knew she was dying and never once came to me and said she was sorry or I love you just the way you are.

I'd never get the approval I'd secretly been craving for years. It was fucked up to know that this is how our story would end. Until the day I died, I'd live knowing that my mother truly did hate me. How do I carry around that burden? I wouldn't be able to. I couldn't. The reality of it was way too cruel and it hurt like hell. My life would never be the same.

I couldn't go on living normally. I couldn't even function enough to book my flight home. I was so distraught; Blue had to charter me a private plane. He was going to come with me but I insisted he stay. If he missed one event his entire schedule would be thrown off. I would be gone for at least a week or more anyway. There was no way I was going to let him take that much time off of work for me. When I boarded the plane he kissed me for what seemed like an eternity.

I didn't want to leave Blue's arms but I had to. I squeezed him tight and promised to call as soon as I landed.

Blue reluctantly let me go and watched as my plane took off. I could tell that he really wanted to come and support me but I needed a minute to myself to process everything. Plus I would be so busy planning the funeral that I wouldn't have time for him anyway. My mother's funeral was packed. She was well respected in the community so people came out in droves to pay their respect.

By the time the repast came I was over shaking hands and pretending like I was holding up well. I was too seconds away from having a nervous breakdown. I felt suffocated in the house full of people. Tee-Tee hadn't stopped crying. My Aunt Candy kept chain smoking and pouring out shots of Jack Daniels on the floor for all of her deceased homies. ZaShontay was walking around looking like one of Uncle Luke's dancers.

Folks were coming up to me left and right giving me their condolences but I didn't want it. Half of the people there didn't even like me. I didn't need their fake ass prayers and well wishes. All I wanted was my mama back. I had to get away from all the chaos so I headed upstairs. Since I'd moved back to St. Louis I hadn't been on the third floor of my mothers' house. It had been ten years since I'd last been up there.

It felt nostalgic to walk up the long flight of stairs. When I was a little girl, I remember sliding down the banister when it was time for breakfast. You know my fat ass couldn't wait to eat. My mom had redecorated a lot. None of the rooms were the same. Tee-Tee's room had been transferred into a sitting room. The only room that remained the same was mine.

My eyes grew wide as I stepped into my childhood room. Everything was exactly the same way I left it. My mother hadn't changed a thing. My old white daybed, pink curtains, television, Baby Sitter's Club books and posters were all still there. It was like a shrine to me. My eyes filled with tears. Maybe I had gotten my mother wrong. Maybe she did love me in her own special way.

This was proof of it. All of my trophies, certificates, Girl Scott badges were displayed in a glass case along with articles written about me over the years. My mother was proud of me. A smiled graced the corners of my lips as I found a throwback picture of me and my mom. I looked to be about three. She held me on her hip and was staring at me with nothing but pure joy and love in her eyes. I gazed at the picture for what felt like hours.

"Can I come in?" I heard someone from behind say.

I was so entranced in the phone that I didn't even recognize the voice. It was Damon. I hadn't seen him at the funeral or burial so it was a surprise to see his face.

"Yeah," I replied, placing the picture back down.

"Damn this brings back memories." He looked around in awe. "Remember when I use to sneak up here with you?"

"That was a long time ago," I responded dryly.

"How are you holding up?" He asked, unbuttoning his suit jacket.

"Barely. I can't get over the fact she's gone."

"Me either. I though your mother would out live us all," Damon joked.

"Me too."

"I know this might not be the right time but I wanted to apologize to you again for what happened. I should've let you know how I was feeling instead of keeping you in the dark."

"It's fine. I'm over it." I waved it off.

"Yeah, I see you all over the blogs and magazines wit' your new man. Who are you dating again? French Montana? No he's dating one of those Kardashian's. Your dude is named after a Crayola crayon, right," Damon joned.

"I'm not about to play with you. You know his name. You can stop with the insults 'cause it's not funny," I spat annoyed.

"You getting mad? You must really like this dude," Damon scoffed.

"I do."

"You like him more than you like me?" He stepped closer.

"Yeah, I do." I stepped back.

"C'mon stop lying. You don't mean that."

"Okay if that's what you wanna tell yourself." I rolled my eyes.

"Sunday, we both know the truth." Damon took me by my arms. "You still love me. I still love you. We can make this work."

"That's just it." I jerked my arms away.

"I don't want to make it work. There's nothing for us to work out. I've moved on. I finally have someone good in my life and I'm not going to fuck that up for you or nobody else. Now if you'll excuse me." I tried to walk past him but Damon stopped me.

Before I knew it he'd wrapped me up in his arms and pushed my back against the wall.

"Damon let me go." I said not in the mood.

Here I was mourning the death of my mother and this nigga was on some old soap opera, Days of Our Lives shit.

"Look me in the eyes and tell me you don't love me."

I looked Damon square in the eyes. I wanted to tell him that I didn't love him anymore but that would be a lie. He'd always have a small piece of my heart. But what I'd experienced with Blue outweighed any feelings I could ever have for Damon.

"See you can't even say it. Just give me one more chance." He kissed me softly on my cheek. "Isabel and I are done for good." He kissed me on the other. "I'm going through with the divorce."

"Good for you. Now move!" I tried to push him away but to no avail.

"Sunday, I love you." He kissed me feverishly on the lips.

I couldn't even front. His lips tasted like sweet sin. I wanted more.

"Let me show you how much I do." Damon slid his hand up my skirt.

His tongue began to dance with mine. Hold up. What the fuck am I doing? This nigga is the devil. Don't get caught up in his web of bullshit again, Sunday.

"Move Damon." I pushed him off of me forcefully.

"I told you, I'm done. Now leave me the fuck alone." I spat leaving him standing there.

If Damon didn't get it before, hopefully he understood now. I was completely over him. I would never go back to him. He and I were over for good. I'd gotten a taste of real pure love. I wouldn't trade that in for the foolishness Damon had to offer. With Blue was where I wanted to be and where I belonged.

Don't let this shit come between us. I'm wrong, you're right.

-Chris Brown, "I Can't Win"

Chapter 22

"I'm happy to have you back." Blue kissed me lovingly on the forehead.

Once I'd squared away everything with my mother, I headed on the first flight back to him. I didn't want to be without him for another second. I never realized how much I needed Blue until I was without him. The man brought out the best in me. Only goodness came from him. Moments like the one we were sharing right now was what I lived for.

We lay face to face in his hotel room doing nothing but basking in the essence of one another. I could look at his handsome face all day. Blue had become my savior. I craved everything about him. With him, I'd begun to see what real love was like. Everything about him was patient, understanding and kind. Nothing between us was ever forced.

We flowed together like water. At night when I cried over missing my mother he held me in his arms. Blue didn't care if he had to be up at the crack of dawn the next morning. He'd stay awake all night long until I finally cried myself to sleep. I thanked god for him. Sometimes, I felt like I wasn't deserving of a love like this.

It was all I'd ever wanted and more but it seemed too good to be true. I couldn't help but wonder when the ball was gonna drop and I'd be left broken hearted. Words couldn't describe my feelings for Blue. I thought that what I shared with Damon was real but that was child's play. Loving Damon was toxic. Only negativity came from being with him.

With Blue everything was smooth sailing. He made me see that I was free to be anything I wanted to be. I actually liked myself when I was with him. I loved the woman I was becoming because of him.

"Where is this food at? A nigga is starving." Blue's stomach growled.

"Me too," I said famished.

"You talk to your brother today?" Blue played with my hair.

"Yeah, he told me he had a rough night last night. But he's holding up well. He's still mad that my mother left my grandmother Dahl's, dining room table to me," I chuckled. "He wanted it so bad. I still can't believe that she left it to me. My mother was one complicated woman. I'll never quite understand her."

"She sounds a lot like you." Blue tickled my stomach.

"Stop!" I laughed hysterically.

"Yo" Blue stopped tickling me. "Don't ever leave me for that long. I was starting to feel some type a way."

"Aww you missed me," I cheesed.

"A lil' bit. Don't let the shit go to your head." Blue replied as there was a knock on the door.

"Look at god," I smiled.

Our food had arrived.

"Thank you Jesus." Blue hopped out of the bed.

I was about to murder the goat cheese pasta I'd ordered. After tipping the room service attendant, Blue joined me at the dining room table. We said grace then proceeded to demolish our food.

"You ready for your show tonight?" I asked opening my bottle of Sprite.

"Yeah, it's sold out. It's gon' be a packed house. I changed some things around in my set so I can't wait to see how the crowd is gonna react."

"I can't wait to see it myself. I hate that I missed your rehearsals." I took a long gulp of the cold drink.

The Sprite hit the spot. Blue and I ate in silence. The food was so good that neither one of us could speak. Full, I sat back and picked up my phone. I hadn't been on Instagram all day. Sometimes, I thought I was addicted to IG. I normally checked in to see what was going on at least ten times a day. I scrolled through my timeline and saw pics of Rihanna showing her titties, T.I. and Tiny throwing subliminal shots at one another and Kermit the Frog telling everybody's business. Tee-Tee had posted a pic of my niece in the cutest little pink tutu. I wanted to pinch her little chubby fat cheeks through the phone.

"Aww look at my niece." I passed Blue my phone. "Ain't she cute?"

Blue looked at the picture and smiled.

"Yeah, she is." He agreed as a text message came through on my phone.

Blue read the message. His face immediately turned to stone. His eyebrows furrowed as he glared at the screen. I didn't know what he was reading but from the look on his face, he was pissed. My heart raced so fast I thought it was going to fall out of my chest.

"What? What's wrong?" I panicked.

"What the fuck is this nigga doing texting you?" He said sharply.

"Who?" I screwed up my face confused.

"Damon, that's who," Blue handed me my phone. "So ya'll kissed?"

I swallowed hard. What in the hell had this nigga text me? I looked down at my screen and read the message.

Today 4:47PM

U can pretend like u don't love me but that kiss said
it all

What the hell? What the fuck doesn't this nigga
get? I don't want him. Why couldn't he just leave me
alone? This was the last thing I wanted to deal with.

"Blue chill. It's not even what you think." I tried to
explain.

"Did you kiss him?" He barked.

I wanted to lie but I could never lie to Blue. I
respected him too much.

"I did but it wasn't like what you're thinking," I
reasoned.

"What could it be then Sunday?" Blue's upper lip
curled.

"He kissed me. I didn't kiss him."

"You kissed him back though right?" Blue sat back
in his seat, heated.

"For a brief second." My voice cracked. "I swear to god it meant nothing, though."

"That's why you didn't want me to come to your mother's funeral 'cause you knew that nigga was gonna be there."

"No that's not true. I wanted you there, I swear." I tried to make him see.

"Yeah, a'ight," Blue liked his bottom lip. "You got me over here lookin' stupid than a muthafucka. Here I am loving you, showing you how a woman is supposed to be treated and you out here kissing another man. Man please, go head wit' that."

"Blue I told him that it was over between us and that I love you. I wouldn't fuck up what we have for nothing. Damon is so last season."

"Apparently not, you up here at ya' mama's funeral kissing him and shit. Yo," Blue massaged his jaw. "We need to fall back."

"What?" My heart stopped beating. "Babe, you're overreacting." I reached over to take his hand but Blue slid his hand off the table.

"I swear to god you are. I'm telling you the truth. The kiss meant nothing to me."

But my words weren't working. I could feel him slipping away. All of the air in my lungs was evaporating.

"Nah, I'm not overreacting. No matter how you try to spin it you still kissed him. Like he said, that says it all. Ain't shit else need to be said. I'm over here playin' chess and you playin' checkers. You ain't ready for a nigga like me. This shit right here proves it. You still caught up on bullshit. You still out here chasing a dream, you ain't gon' never catch."

This can not be fucking happening to me. Blue was breaking up with me. Yeah, I was wrong for even letting Damon near me but my love for Blue was true. I was done with Damon but the question still remained. Why had I kissed him? Maybe it was my way of sabotaging myself. I wasn't used to being happy. I'd never truly been before. All I knew was drama.

Peace obviously didn't work for me. But as I stood there witnessing the demise of my relationship, I realized that all I wanted was peace. I wanted a peaceful, loving

303

relationship with Blue. I couldn't lose him now. He was my life vest. I needed him like I needed air to breathe.

"You should leave." He finally said.

I closed my eyes and tried my damnedest to make his words go away, to make our argument go away and to make myself disappear. I didn't want to be there anymore. If I didn't have Blue, I had nothing else to live for. I would give my limbs to rewind time to just a few minutes ago when we were lying in bed. We were happy there. I was happy there. Everything about us was good. I had him. He had me. We had it all. Now I had nothing.

You're really gon' make me expose you for what you are.

~Fantasia feat Kelly Rowland

& Missy Elliot, "Without Me"

Chapter 23

Everything I had disappeared. I'd lost everything, my mama, my man, my business and now my sanity. No matter how much I begged and pleaded for Blue to see things my way he didn't. I was sent packing on the first plane back to St. Louis. I was cast away to never be seen or heard from again. Blue was so mad at me that he even changed his number. I'd fucked up but I didn't deserve this kind of punishment.

Once again, I'd come inches away from the finish line only to be pushed back to the start. What the fuck was I doing wrong? I couldn't keep a man for shit. I was so distraught over my break up that I didn't even feel sane enough to be alone. I stayed at Emma's to ensure that I wouldn't do anything crazy. I could feel myself about to snap. One wrong move and somebody was going to get hurt. The kids were at Emma's parents' house so she and I along with Tee-Tee drank ourselves to oblivion. I had to drown my sorrows in alcohol in order not kill anyone.

"Girl, I am not gon' be able to drive home." Tee-Tee lay upside down on the couch on his iPad.

"Hell, John might get some tonight." Emma laughed into her red cup.

"I was getting my back cracked on the regular but now that's all gone," I wept.

"It's going to be ok friend." Emma ruffled my hair with her fingers.

"Lord, I just want him back!" I took a huge gulp of Vodka from my cup."What do I have to do? I'll do anything Jesus! Just point me in the right direction! Blue Ivy bless me!"

"You know whose fault this is don't you?" Emma looked at me and Tee-Tee.

"Who?" We both said in unison.

"Damon. He did this to you." Emma slurred her words.

"You're right," I agreed.

"I had something concrete and now it's all gone and it's because of him. He has ruined my entire life. I hate him." I felt my temperature rise.

I took the bottle of Grey Goose to the head. Flashes of all of Damon's lies and games filled my head. I had to hurt him. He had to pay for taking the last thing that made me happy away.

"Hey no back wash," Tee-Tee shouted.

"Shut up! I bought it." I took another long drink.

"I have to get him back," I announced.

"You do," Emma nodded her profusely. "He can't get away this. We gotta fuck him up. Let's cut his balls off then throw them in the Mississippi river." Emma sneered devilishly.

"Nah, that's not good enough," I shook my head. "We gotta hit him where it hurts. Let's cut his penis and his balls off, put it in a meat grinder, make a hamburger patty out of it and serve it to him on a sesame seed bun," I said seriously.

"Yeah, I'm down," Emma's eyes lit up with delight.

"Aww shit!" Tee-Tee sat up straight. "I know where he's at."

"Who?" I asked, taking another drink of Vodka.

"Damon."

"How?"

"Isabel just posted a picture of them together on Facebook." Tee-Tee showed us his iPad.

Everything in my head had officially exploded. A week ago Damon stood in my face and professed his love for me. Now he was at the Pink Hats 40th anniversary party with the woman he claimed he was divorcing. Oh hell no! Damon McKnight was not going to come out of this with his hands clean. If he wanted to ruin my life I was going to ruin his.

"Where my keys at?" I searched around for them.

"Where are you going?" Emma eyed me quizzically.

"I'm going to the party."

"Sunday you're drunk. You're in no shape to drive. I'll drive you," Emma hiccupped.

She was drunker than me.

"We gon' ride on these fools!" I pretended to shoot a gun in the air. "G4L all day, er'day."

"I don't know what that means but yeah," Emma replied amped up.

"I'll stay and man the fort." Tee-Tee confirmed.

It nearly took me and Emma an hour just to find my car keys. Once we did there was no stopping us. It took us fifteen minutes to get to the country club. The entire ride over we continued to drink. By the time we got there I looked a sloppy drunk mess but I didn't care. The liquor had blinded me to reality. I thought I was doing the damn think in my holey Beyoncé tee shirt, ripped jeans and Tims. You couldn't tell me I wasn't the shit. Emma and I barged into the country club like we owned the place.

I pushed open the doors to the banquet room and walked in. There wasn't an empty seat in the place. The who's who of St. Louis was there. Everyone was dressed elegantly in their gowns and tuxedos and here I was looking like a backup dancer for Kesha. I searched the dimly lit room for Damon. It took me a minute but I found him. He sat in the front of the room right next to Isabel.

He had his arm wrapped around her shoulder. The two of them looked like two peas in a pod. Seeing them together made me even angrier. This nigga was a joke. How had I not seen it before? It became officially clear to me at that moment that nothing about us was real. Damon just liked having control over my feelings. To him I was nothing more than the quiet, desperately seeking love, ex fatty that grew up next door. I had to let him know that I was aware of his game.

"Excuse me," I said making my way through the tables.

I was making so much noise that the lights had come up. Emma followed behind me making just as much of a ruckus. Everyone was whispering and staring at us. But we didn't care, fuck'em. I was a woman on a mission. Damon turned in his seat to see what all the commotion was about and connected eyes with me. A look of sheer horror was on his face. Never in a million years did he expect to see me there.

"Sunday, what are you doing here?" He rose from his seat.

"I'm here to do this." I reared my hand back and slapped him clean across the face.

I slapped him so hard that the corner of his mouth had begun to bleed. The entire room gasped. Damn that felt good! I had been wanting to slap a bitch for a while.

"Have you lost your fuckin' mind?" Damon pushed me so hard I almost fell back onto the table behind me.

"Don't put your hands on my husband!" Isabel spat.

"Yeah, don't put your hands on her husband!" Annabelle yelled.

"Security! Escort this crazy woman out of here," Damon demanded.

"Oh so now I'm crazy." I caught my balance. "I wasn't crazy a few weeks ago when you were begging me to take you back."

"What?" Isabel said with a look of distress on her face. "What is she talkin' about Damon?"

"Yeah, what am I talkin' about Damon?" I cocked my head to the side.

"Don't listen to her. She's crazy. Can't you smell the liquor on her breath? She's turning into a drunk just like her mother."

No words had ever cut me so deep. Damon of all people knew first hand my struggles with my mother. He knew how much her drinking bothered me. Now he was going to use my concerns against me? I never hated anyone but at that moment I hated him.

"Like seriously, Sunday you need to pull it together. This obsession of yours with me is becoming a little bit scary," Damon continued on.

"Move out the way! I'ma cut him!" Emma picked up a butter knife and charged towards Damon.

One of the gentlemen at the party stopped her before she could make contact.

"Will somebody get security? They're both crazy!" Damon pleaded.

"I don't know what I ever saw in you." Salty tears strolled down my cheeks.

I wasn't crying because Damon was trying to play me out in front of everyone. I cried for my mother. She didn't deserve to be disrespected like that.

"Sunday we had a thing going in high school but its over. I love my wife. You need to understand that and move on. I would hate to have to put a restraining order out on you." Damon talked to me like I was a mental patient.

"Chile please, if I don't put one out on you first. For whatever foolish reason, I really believed that you loved me but you don't. You don't love me. You don't love Isabel either. The only person you love is yourself. You never had any intentions on divorcing her, did you?" I got up in his face and pointed my finger at his head like a gun.

"Divorce?" Isabel stood up. "Since when were we getting a divorce? You told me you just needed time to think things over. Never once did you mention a divorce."

"Girl, he's been playing the both of us." I shook my head. "I'm so glad I called off our engagement."

"Hold up." Isabel put her hand up as if to say freeze. "Pause. That was real? Damon told me that you just made that up to get back at me for what happened at the spa. He told me that you all had messed around a few times in the past but that it was over."

"How was it over when I was staying at Damon's crib?" I eyed Damon up and down. "Explain that Damon."

"Yo' she's crazy. Don't believe her." Damon grabbed Isabel by her arms. "She's just mad that I don't want her. Don't let her fuck up what we have."

"You told me you lived there alone." Isabel pushed him in the chest.

She was starting to realize that her husband wasn't shit.

"Isabel, I was around your girls on the 4th of July," I confirmed.

"I know that but he made it seem like you were on some stalker ish. He said that you came over with Emma uninvited. He said that he didn't even want you there but was too afraid to ask you to leave 'cause he thought you

315

might do something to yourself." Tears fell from Isabel's eyes.

"All this time I thought you were just going through a little mini mid life crisis or something. You made me feel like I was crazy, like I was a nag or some of kind of burden on you. Oh my god," she gasped.

"That's why you always wanted to come to the house to see the girls 'cause she was there." Isabel put two and two and together.

"Let's jump him." Mirabel popped her knuckles.

"He told me that you wouldn't let the girls come over. His ass has been pitting us against each other this whole time. He's been making us look like some damn fools," I concluded.

"How could you do this?" Isabel sobbed. "We have a family. We have a baby on the way."

"Wheeeet?" I said stunned by her revelation.

I didn't see that one coming at all.

"Yo' trifling ass moved out of our home so you could whore around and openly cheat on me?!" Isabel yelled.

"Wow…" I shook my head. "You are a piece of shit. God bless my mother's soul 'cause she told me about you. She was right all along."

"I was too," Emma chimed in.

"You are the master manipulator. You never loved me. I was just a lil' play thing for you but not any more sweetie. Isabel, thank you for getting pregnant with Gia on purpose. I wouldn't want to be in your shoes for all the Chanel in the world. "

"Is that what you told her?" Isabel's bottom lip quivered. "You got me pregnant on purpose 'cause you said you wanted me to have your baby!"

"This is ridiculous." Emma said in disbelief.

"Umm can you all please take this outside?" The M.C. asked over the microphone. "We would like to resume with our program.

317

"Oh, I'm done. This piece of shit ass muthafucka will never hear from me again. Isabel he's all yours." I bowed out as gracefully as a drunken woman could.

"I don't want his ass either. We're getting a divorce!" Isabel shot past him and stormed out.

Mirabel and Annabelle ran behind her.

"Isabel wait!" Damon jogged after her.

"Looks like our job here is done." I slapped fives with Emma.

"They wasn't ready," Emma bragged, picking up someone's roll and taking a bite out of it.

"You folks have a nice night." I said to everyone in the room. "And please, in the words of Tina Turner, don't get nothin' on ya'. Mama," I looked up at the ceiling. "That was for you."

∫

I want your heart, love and emotions, endlessly.
-Drake, "Hold On We're

Going Home"

Chapter 24

For weeks, the city buzzed about my epic showdown with Damon at the Pink Hats 40th Anniversary Party. As word spread, all sorts of women came out of the woodwork saying that they'd been sleeping with Damon too. Apparently this low life had been on some Tiger Woods shit. He had chicks all over St. Louis that he was dickin' down. I was sick to my stomach. I immediately got tested for all venereal diseases and HIV.

Thankfully they all came back negative. Dealing with Damon taught me a huge lesson. Never again would I disregard my gut intuition. My conscious was telling me that something wasn't right with him but I ignored every sign. At all costs, I had to make my fairytale come true. I was so desperate to be married and a mother that I was willing to ignore all the warnings signs just to get what I wanted.

Since moving back to St. Louis, I'd completely wrecked my life. I'd gone from being a functioning human being that contributed to society to a lovesick nutcase. After taking the time out to reflect, I soon realized why my love life was a failure. I was so busy trying to find Mr. Right that I didn't find myself. No man would ever love me if I didn't love myself.

I invested too much of my existence and my happiness in the men that I was dating. If I didn't have somebody in my life, I felt incomplete and that was a problem. I should complete me. A man should just be an extension of my happiness. I had to get myself together. I had to truly love myself before I could expect a man to love me.

In order to do so I decided to move back to L.A. I had to get my life back on track there alone. I didn't want to lean on my family and friends. I wanted to lean on myself. I needed to have my own back for once. My family understood but was disappointed to see me leave, especially Emma. She cried like a baby.

I swore to her that she had nothing to worry about. Unlike when I moved to L.A the first time, this time I had every intention on keeping in touch. She was my bestie. I wasn't going to dare let our friendship slip through my fingers again. I was going to make a conscious effort to visit at least three or four times a year. It wouldn't be ten years before anybody saw me again.

Three months had passed and I was back in L.A. I was on grind mode. *Two Hearts L.A* was thriving. I was back in my element. When I wasn't working my ass off, I did hot yoga, took long walks on the beach and read a lot of self help books. After spending so much time alone I actually began to enjoy my own company. I came to find out that I was a pretty cool chick to be around. Although, I adored myself, I couldn't ignore the constant yearning for Blue to be back in my life.

I hadn't seen nor heard from him in months. He'd completely shut me out. I had no idea how to reach out to him. Hell, I didn't even think he would want to hear from me. Maybe it was best we stay apart. I didn't want to bring anymore unnecessary drama to his life.

Before I knew it 2014 was coming to an end. It was New Years Eve and I was back where I started, in the club. I don't know why I didn't just stay my ass at home and watch the ball drop like every other lonely bitch in America. For some reason, I decided to get dressed up and go out by my damn self.

I felt beautiful in my charcoal, Donna Karen, belted, sheer organza, halter cocktail dress. A cute pair of Valentino strappy sandals and a Rebecca Minkoff clutch enhanced my look. I was having fun sipping on a glass of champagne until I noticed that everyone around me was boo'd up. Partying solo instantly wasn't so much fun anymore. Suddenly, the loud music and neon lights had started to make my head hurt. Then things went from bad to worse. I spotted Blue and his people across the room in the V.I.P. section. I could've sworn he spotted me too but I wasn't sure.

Blue looked amazing as always. I'd never seen him so dressed up in person. He donned a black Tom Ford suit, white shirt, black tie and Lanvin shoes. I wanted nothing more than to walk over to him and say hi but I didn't want to embarrass myself. If he dissed me in front of his friends, I'd never show my face in L.A. again so I decided to fall back. Plus it was almost midnight. I did not want to be there when the clock struck twelve.

What if Blue kissed another chick in front of me? I wouldn't be able to stomach it. Nope, it was time for me to leave. I should've stayed my black ass home in the first place. What was I thinking? I know better than to do dumb shit like this. Sunday, take your ass home and get in the bed. I quickly took another sip of champagne and glanced over at Blue once more. This time there was no denying it. He was looking my way.

We caught eyes and stared at one another for what felt like an eternity. *I should go over and say hi,* I thought. Maybe he missed me too. I wouldn't find out if I didn't say anything to him. Just when I was about to build up the courage to go over and speak, Blue turned his face and started talking to some girl. I was devastated. He was over me. Seeing him all up in the girls face proved it. I had to get out of there.

The countdown to the New Year was just about to begin. I would be damned if I let any of them drunk fools in the club see me ruin my makeup with tears. Inside my car, I placed my head on the steering wheel and cried like a baby. I cried for myself, my mother and for fucking up my relationship with Blue. Wiping my face with the back of my hand, I looked at the clock. It was 11:50p.m. I was not about to begin my new year in the parking lot.

Pulling myself together, I placed my keys into the ignition and sped off. A few seconds later, I stopped at a red light. It was 11:53p.m. I'd failed at reaching my goal of being married by the end of the year but it was ok. I didn't need a man to complete me. I was good by myself. I would go through with IVF and have my baby alone.

As I accepted my fate, I heard a car horn blow behind me. The driver was blowing their horn non-stop. I looked through my rearview mirror to see who it was. I couldn't tell who the driver was because of their head lights. I looked in my driver side mirror and spotted Blue hopping out of his car.

My heart skipped a beat and I stopped breathing. This was not happening. Blue walked up to my car and opened the door. I looked at him breathlessly. Blue took me by the hand and helped me out of the car.

"Who told you to leave without telling me?" He asked with a stone expression on his face.

"I thought you were with that girl, that's why I didn't say hello," I replied, trying to steady my breathing.

"That's my new assistant Chantell."

"Oh..." I said taking in the information.

Blue looked down at me and I looked up at him. I'd imagine this moment for months and now that it was here I was speechless. He was there, standing right in front of me in the middle of the street. It wasn't a dream. This was my reality. Cars behind us were honking their horns because the light had turned green. I couldn't hear the car horns. All I heard was the sound of my heart beating out of my chest.

"Blue I'm sorry," I apologized. "I never meant to hurt you. You gotta understand that there was nothing going on between me and Damon."

"I know. Dylan told me," he confessed.

I wanted to ask him a million questions, like when did Dylan tell him? Why hadn't he called? But none of that mattered. I had to cease the moment. I had to tell him how I felt. It might be my only chance.

"Blue, I miss you. I love you and if you'll give me another chance I swear to god—"

"Shut up." He pulled me close. "It's midnight." He planted his lips on mine and kissed me fervently.

My entire body became weak. Thank you god.

"I love you too," Blue gazed deep into my eyes.

"Happy New Year, Blue."

"Happy New Year."

92118755R00182

Made in the USA
Lexington, KY
29 June 2018